In Pursuit of a Dream

by Dennis Doane

RoseDog✤Books
PITTSBURGH, PENNSYLVANIA 15238

The contents of this work, including, but not limited to, the accuracy of events, people, and places depicted; opinions expressed; permission to use previously published materials included; and any advice given or actions advocated are solely the responsibility of the author, who assumes all liability for said work and indemnifies the publisher against any claims stemming from publication of the work.

All Rights Reserved
Copyright © 2021 by Dennis Doane

No part of this book may be reproduced or transmitted, downloaded, distributed, reverse engineered, or stored in or introduced into any information storage and retrieval system, in any form or by any means, including photocopying and recording, whether electronic or mechanical, now known or hereinafter invented without permission in writing from the publisher.

RoseDog Books
585 Alpha Drive
Suite 103
Pittsburgh, PA 15238
Visit our website at *www.rosedogbookstore.com*

ISBN: 978-1-6470-2098-9
eISBN: 978-1-6470-2074-3

Contents

Chapter One	1
Chapter Two	11
Chapter Three	21
Chapter Four	27
Chapter Five	39
Chapter Six	47
Chapter Seven	49
Chapter Eight	53
Chapter Nine	61
Chapter Ten	65
Chapter Eleven	77
Chapter Twelve	87
Chapter Thirteen	105

Chapter One

Monty Lane was in love with the most beautiful woman in all of Texas. No, she was more beautiful than any woman in the whole world. In his eyes anyway. And He knew she was in love with him. He was sure of it. The only problem was that Monty couldn't marry her,… not just yet anyway. Why couldn't she understand it?.. Oh, it wasn't because he didn't want to marry her, he did. Very much so!

With all of his heart, he wanted to marry her. Was he really in love with her? you bet you're pointed toe boots he was in love with her. That he was sure of! Actually she was the only girl he had ever loved…at least that he wanted to marry. But in spite of all of his deep feelings for Beth, he just couldn't do it… Not right now!

And, Yes, he was definitely convinced of her love for him. That she was in love with no other, but him. He knew that too! You just couldn't look in each other's eyes the way they did and not know and feel love. You couldn't hold one another in your arms and not feel such deep love. Yes, he wanted to marry her right now, but there was some-thing he must do first. And until he did, in spite of his love for her and hers for him, this thing would always stand between them. Oh, she would not think so, at least right now, but it would bother him. And regardless of how deep his love was for her, and hers for him, he just couldn't marry her right now. But Monty believed he had the answer to this problem that kept them apart.

All he had to do was to convince Beth of his plan, then carry it out! In his mind it was a simple solution…if he could persuade Beth to agree. Now that was going to take some doing. Not only was Beth pretty, she was a smart, and determined lady. And once she had her mind settled on something it was some difficult to change it. However, she would not admit that. This he knew because he had tried to change it. The big problem was that when he did try to change her mind and she refused to agree with him in the matter…she was right! Once or twice she had reminded him of that. And she was not going agree with him now. She was going to tell him he was just being silly.

Was he? Was it his male ego that kept him from, "popping the question"?

When she looked into his eyes, and he searched hers, when her lips so gently touched his, and they were both embraced in each other's arms there was no doubt in Monty's heart that Beth loved him. And she was probably right, he possibly was being silly… This thing that held them apart. And he must be careful not to let this monster inside of him keep them apart forever. Maybe Beth was right. Maybe he should put this thing aside. But, no, he just couldn't. Everytime he tried to put it aside, it rose up its ugly head. Why, did independence mean so much to him, as a man? Maybe it didn't mean that much to some men but it did to him. And Beth had been so patient with him. Bethany tried to understand Monty's reasoning, but she just couldn't. All this hesitation just because she had inherited a cattle ranch of over 50,000 acres stocked with several thousand head of prime beef when her father died. And all of the ranch buildings were in top shape. And her ranch hands all "rode for the brand." Monty reasoned with himself about the matter and just could not think of a single worthwhile offering he could bring or add to their marriage. All Monty could add to this marriage was one stallion, one gelding, a well worn saddle, one long gun, and a pair of colts. That's it! And that just wasn't enough! Bethany tried to reason with him that it was his love for her that made all the difference in the world. But Monty just couldn't erase the rumors he thought he could hear that people were saying, "Boy, that Monty Lane sure married well." He would instantly become a rich man when he married Beth Hase!" Yes sir, he would have it made. " People just wouldn't believe he was only a hired hand, like all the other hands on the ranch. And they were all correct! He was more than just a "hired hand." The more he thought about it the worse he thought about himself. Why couldn't he be content with just being a hired hand anyway? Why couldn't people understand it wasn't Beth's money or ranch he was after. It was Beth he loved, It was Beth he wanted, not her ranch! And he couldn't ask Beth to give it all up for him and go elsewhere. Nor could he just ride off and leave this woman either. He loved her! He had never met a girl like her. Often when he was away on the trail of steers or wild mustangs, or on a roundup he had to force himself to keep his mind on his work. When the day was done and he was sleeping on the ground with his head resting against his saddle, he would fall asleep thinking about her. When he would get back to the ranch and she would come running to meet him he would dismount before his horse stopped and sweep her up in his arms and return the kiss she so eagerly pressed against his lips. So many times the hands would say to him, "Why don't you marry that girl, Monty?" Monty would say, he wanted to but he had nothing to bring to bring to the marriage. Sometimes, they would answer him with, "who you marrying boy, that girl or people and their opinions?" They were right, of course. And so was Beth. This couldn't go on. It just couldn't! She was the only woman he had ever loved. Bethany was the only woman he had ever felt this way about. These were trying and gloomy days for Monty Lane. He was just a hired hand on the Circle B! A forty dollar a month cowhand and she was his boss. And a wealthy one at that. He just couldn't erase that! So, he had to learn to live with it!

Something else haunted Monty too. Monty Lane had not lost his dream about his horse ranch. A dream that dated back to when he was just a kid in West Texas. He had spent all of his life around horses. He could ride about anything with hair. Well, almost anything. That didn't mean he wouldn't get tossed. But he was a determined man. He would get back on and ride until he either broke the horse to ride or it busted him up so bad he couldn't get back on. So far that hadn't happened. True, it was tempting to toss his pride overboard and marry the boss. She sure was a beautiful woman. But she was not only beautiful she had the best personality to go with her beauty. To Monty she was one of a kind…and if he had to give up on his dream of his horse ranch in order to be her intended….then so be it!

Being married to Beth meant more to him than anything. But, he also had been dreaming of a way that he could start a horse ranch along with her cattle ranch. And he could make it pay too. He knew he could. Right now there were thousands of good wild stock running loose and free over the plains just waiting to be caught and gentled. They had been running free since the days Cortez reached the coast of Mexico. At times Monty would think about the days when Cortez, with his eleven ships landed and how the people must have reacted to seeing these strange animals being used in different ways. They must have spent a lot of time watching the ways man and horse worked together. They were amazed at how horse and man worked together. If it worked for the Spaniards it could work for them as well. The advantage of the horse spread rapidly and the indian quickly adapted to using them. They became experts in their use of the horse.

When the Pueblo indians drove the Spaniards from the Santa Fe- Albuquerque region, they also left several thousand horses. It wasn't long until these indians were breeding them and maintaining even larger herds. They sold them to surrounding tribes like the Apache and the Comanches. All of this resulted in changing the life style of the Indian forever. It couldn't help but to change their way of life too. And it changed the way of the white man as well.

The horse made it much easier to hunt and kill the buffalo. Their means of travel and moving from place to place was much easier with the use of the horse.

And of course the taming and the use of the horse was a great advantage in warfare.

Over the years the wild horse herds were increased by horses that had escaped from trappers, explorers, pioneers, miners, ranchers, and even the U.S. Cavalry. Sometimes it was deliberate like during the Civil War, it had been rumored that the US cavalry released good Morgan, Arabian, and Thoroughbred stallions into the roaming wild herds to improve the horse herds. They would later recapture those selected from the herds for their own use. The result of all of this, with the help of natural selection, worked together to produce an intelligent, sound-minded, surefooted and strong mustang that roamed the west in the tens of thousands. Monty remembered his daddy telling him he bet there were over a million wild horses running loose over the plains. Monty was sure his Black was the result of such exceptional breeding. His stallion was one of those "too good to be true" horses that had been running free over the plains.

However with the coming of farmers, and ranchers, springing up with small towns in the west, there also came small farms and gardens with fences. Many of these small ranches came with fences…barb wire. The barbed wire fences made a change in the west as well as the small towns and stage coaches. All of this helped to cut down the open range of the Great Plains. Sometimes range wars and fence wars were fought over these boundaries. Thank goodness Monty had escaped all of that. Monte Lane was greatfull he didn't have to deal with all of that. But he knew he could make a horse ranch pay. There would always be a demand for good horse flesh. And right now, there it was, free. If he could build and stock a good horse ranch then he would have something worthwhile to offer Beth, the woman he loved. Then no one would be able to accuse him of marrying Beth Hase for her ranch. No one!

And if Monte knew anything, he knew horses. He knew breeds, what to look for in choosing a horse with staying power, and he knew horse savvy. But, no sir, he just couldn't marry Beth any other way. It just wasn't right. He had to bring something to her now, in the beginning. And right now he just didn't have it. Not yet anyway. But he felt sure it was coming. He just felt it. It was coming! He was certain of it. But until it happened he had to wait… He just hoped Beth would wait and not grow too impatient with him. To make matters worse he saw her most everyday. Sometimes it was about all he could do to restrain himself. And she didn't help matters much. Only Monty didn't realize that Beth saw the way he looked at her. Nathan, the ramrod, also knew, plus most of the hands. Beth knew Monty deliberately avoided her at times for his own reasons. She knew he cared for her and she was ready to be his wife, if only he would ask her. And if he wouldn't, then she had to find a way to persuade him. Yes, she could find a way. And you can bet she would!

With all of this running through his mind, Monty turned his horse on to the main street of town of Ludwig, he couldn't help noticing a large banner strung in front of the "Suds" Saloon. It was advertising an upcoming county horse race. The prize money was $3,000. Monty turned his black gelding, Blackjack, toward the hitching post and swung out of the saddle. He pushed his way through the bat wing doors of the saloon and walked up to the bar. The bartender, Gabby, met him with a glass and asked what he would have. To his obvious disappointment Monty replied,"right now just a little information."

Monty quickly decided that it might be best to invest in the bartender's good graces, so, he took reach into his shirt pocked and produced enough money to cover the drink and tossed it on the bar and said, "Give me a cold beer, to start." The bartender winked at 3 cowboys sitting at a table nearby and said, "Why sure cowboy." He then produced a bottle and poured Monty's glass three fingers full. Monty tossed it down and made an ugly face. The cowboys and the bartender all laughed. "What's the matter cowboy, that not cold enough for you?" Monty laughed, held up his glass and asked for another. The bartender said to him as he set his glass down, "This time just sip it cowboy." Monty held his shot glass up and winked at the bartender as he took a sip. He set his glass down and grinned at the bartender and asked about information on the upcoming race. Well, it was two weeks away and it would be run at the edge of town where a temporary race track was being built. Entrance fee was $500, payable within ten days. $500 was a lot of money to Monty. Where was he going to get that kind of money?

A tall slender cowboy from the nearby table spoke up, "If your thinking on ridding in that race you might as well save your money, cowboy!" "So what makes you think I can't win," asked Monty? "Cause ole man Bracket's son, Jed, is going to race that new stallion his daddy just bought him. He's supposed to be the fastest horse in these parts. The way I hear it, there's not anything on four legs that can catch him."

The second cowboy spoke up and said, " Besides that Jed is a sore loser, and if "ya" did win "ole" Jed would most likely shoot you… Dead! He packs a lot feeling and pride in that black stallion. But mostly, Jed just doesn't like to lose… at anything … to anyone." "Shoot a man for winning a horse race fair and square? Come-on, the sheriff would have him for murder," said Monty. "Ha," laughed the third cowboy. "That ole man Bracket's got that sheriff in his hip pocket and a lot other folks in this town, like the town banker." He sat his beer down and wiped his mouth on his faded red shirt sleeve.

Just then the batwing doors pushed open and in stepped a young fancy dressed cowboy wearing dark pants, expensive looking polished boots, a light blue shirt, and a black and white cowhide vest. He sported a thin dark mustache across his upper lip. He also wore a tied down pearl handled colt on his right hip. He strutted up to the bar and ordered "whisky." After he tossed his drink he grinned at the three cowboys and said, "Well, I see the three town clowns are still lazing around in the saloon this afternoon. What no good are you three up to today?" The tall skinny cowboy had a grin on his face as he said, "we were just talking to this cowboy who wants to race against that stallion of yours, in this upcoming race. He thinks he just might win."

The grin suddenly vanished from Jed's face as he turned toward Monty. "That true stranger?" "I'm no stranger," said Monty. " I ride for the Circle B. And yes, I was talking about entering that race. It's open to the public."

Jed had an instant dislike for this stranger. It was evident that he didn't know the Bracket name in this town. He looked at this stranger up and down and then said, "Mister you don't stand a ghost of a chance. That black stallion of mine will run anything on four legs right into the ground."

"Well," said Monty, "I believe I'll risk it."

"Mister I just told you to back off. I decide who races against me, and you ain't welcome, so go on back to your cows. He sniffed lightly and grinned as he said, "You even smell like one." A smirk now appeared on Jed's face as his right hand dropped down to his six shooter.

Monty recognized the challenge and stiffened up, his right hand down by his side right near his colt. He said "If I choose to ride in that race, you sure won't stop me, junior." "Who you calling junior?" Jed answered angrily as he squared off toward Monty as if he was ready to draw." At that moment the bat wing doors parted and in walked a man carrying a "greener" which suddenly swung hip high as he saw two hombres squared off at each other and ready to draw. There was a shiny tin star on his shirt. "I don't know what's going on here, but, Jed, you back off. Lane, that means you too." Neither man moved. It was clear that a new grudge match had just been born. Jed was just itching to prove he was the better man and Monte was confident of his draw. Sheriff, Ben Baker was the new sheriff. He surprised both Hale and Bracket by his sudden entrance at this particular moment. Bracket was surprised at the timing and Lane that he knew his name. Sheriff Baker said to each man again, "I mean it, I'll drill the first one who draws with a load of buckshot, now back off, both of you," Jed glared at the new sheriff and then slung himself around toward the bar. The sheriff turned toward Monty and asked what was going on. Monty replied, "Nothing I couldn't handle." "That's not what I asked," replied the sheriff. One of the cowboys spoke up and said," This gent said he was going to enter this upcoming race and it made Jed mad."

The sheriff looked at Jed and said, "I'm telling you Jed Bracket to stop that interfering with this race or I'll lock you up and you won't race at all. You understand me? It's none of your affair who rides in that race. You understand me?"

Jed wheeled toward the new sheriff and angrily said, "I'm going to tell my dad about this and come the next sheriff's election you'll be out of a job mister." "Maybe so," but your daddy has already talked to me and told me to hold you in check, so back off Jed." He then turned to Monty and said. "Mr. Lane, if your business here is done I'd suggest you be on your way so there won't be any more trouble."

Monty looked at Jed, his anger still brewing inside him. Jed had no idea how close he had been to death. Monty then looked at the sheriff. He had already figured out his next move so he tipped his hat at the sheriff and left. Once outside he patted his horse , then put his foot in the stirrup and mounted. One of the three gents at the table hollered at the bartender, "Hey can I have what's left of his drink?" The bartender shook his head with a grin and shoved it toward him.

Monty headed Blackjack toward the telegram office. Upon his arrival he greeted the station officer then asked about sending a telegraph. The telegrapher's black office cap was tipped back on his head, he grabbed a pencil from beside his ear and a piece of paper and said to Monty, "shoot." He then glanced down at the twin guns Lane had strapped around his waist, cleared his throat, and smiled faintly and said, "I mean tell me what you want me to send." Monty dictated the words to him and the message was sent. It was a telegram to a lawyer friend, Jesse Brown, back in his home county instructing him to sell his home place and wire the money to him as quickly as he could. He then mounted Blackjack and headed for the ranch.

He said nothing to Nathan about his brush with Jed or his sending the telegraph.

Two weeks later a rider rode up to the ranch with a telegram for Monty. Now everyone was interested in a telegram, so Nathan and two of the new hands, Zeke Gage, and Rife Start gathered around Monty to see if it was good news.

The telegram was from Monty's lawyer friend telling him that his property sold quickly and for more than he thought it would. He had taken out his fee and that the rest of the money had been wired to the Sheriff. Zeke slapped Monty on the back and said, "Boy, Monty, that's got to be a lot of drinking money, let's go into town and collect. We'll have us a 'whingdinger' of a time." "No," said Monty. "That money represents years of hard work by my ma and pa, and me and I'll not waste it on booze." "Sounds like you might have definite plans for that money," said Nathan. "I do," replied Monty. "This is the start of a dream." "Care to share any of that dream with us," asked Zeke. "No, not right now, but maybe someday soon. No one asked him anymore. It was the code of the west. You never pried into another man's business. You waited until he was ready to talk to you and then you listened. But Nathan had a hunch about Monte. Someday, when he found himself, this man was going to stand tall among his peers. From behind Monte came a female voice asking, "what about me, Monty? Can you share it with me?" Nathan kind of jumped and turned, then grinned.

"Well, it concerns you…in a way. Soon, I will discuss it with you. .. I promise."

It wasn't until then that Monty was fully aware that there was a stranger present with Beth. He looked at the pretty young woman following Beth and said to her, "Afternoon ma'am," and he sort of tipped his hat.

Beth quickly apologized for not introducing her friend to Monty. "Monty," She said, "This is my friend, Becky, who lives on a ranch not very far from us. She came over for a visit this afternoon." Then she turned to Vicky and said, "Vicky, this is the man I plan to marry…when we work out all the details."

Vicky smiled as she extended her hand and said, looking at Monty, "Boy Bethany, he is nice looking. If you let him get away there just might be a rush of females chasing him, and I might be one of them." Monty's face turned a little red and managed a smile. Beth gave a controlled smile. It was obvious it was forced. Monty was embarrassed and Beth was not just a little displeased at her remark. Nathan watched Monty and Beth walk away their hands joined, and Vicky walking on the other side of Monty. It looked and sounded like Vicky was trying to carry the conversation, but Beth was refusing to allow Monty's attention to be anywhere but on her. Nathan saw there was more to Monty Lane than just a quick temper and a fast gun. He was good with cattle and better with horses. He also had a way of conducting himself in awkward situations. Just as he was doing now. Vicky was saying to Monty, "Did you grow up around in this region, Monty?"

Monty looked at her and answered, "No, Ma'am. I'm not from anywhere around here."

Vicky, asked, "Well, if you're not from around here, then where? Have you always worked on a ranch? I noticed that you ride well, are you a wrangler?"

Beth, said, "Vicky, he just got home. Give him a chance to catch his breath."

"Oh, I'm sorry Beth. I didn't mean to monopolize him. It's just that I don't know how such a good looking man could have escaped my attention."

Monty didn't know what to say so he just decided to remain silent. Best not to give any information. As he had heard one person say once, "Silence is Golden."

But Vicky just wouldn't quit. After a few moments she said, "Bethany, are you going to the dance next Friday night? If you do, I hope you will bring Monty with you?" Beth answered, "I might," then added, "If Monty feels like going."

"Well, if you do come, Monty, will you save me a dance," she asked. Being caught in the middle of something he was not prepared for, he answered, "We'll see." "Oh, I'll look forward to it," she said. Monty looked at her and said, "We'll see, I said. "No promises."

Vicky looked at Beth and said, "I need to be going now. See you at the dance Bethany, you lucky girl."

With that Vicky took the reins of her horse and placed her foot in the stirrup and very easily and gracefully swung up in the saddle. She waved her hand and smiled broadly as she encouraged her horse off at a gallop. As she galloped off Monty looked at Beth and asked, "where did she come from?"

Before Beth answered, Monty said to her, "And I am not going to that dance."

Beth, looked at Monty with a grin and said, "Monty Lane, are you going to stand there and tell me you didn't enjoy all that sweet talk and attention you were getting?

Monty, took Bethany in his arms and said, "I wanted to be alone with you Beth."

With that this tall shy cowboy took Beth in his arms, looked around then placed a quick kiss on this woman who had captured his heart. Nathan Frame just happened to be standing on the steps on the side steps and he saw them in an embrace. He mumbled to himself an approval of what he was seeing and said to himself, "Beth, you couldn't have made a better choice. Monty has makings of the kind of man the west needs. He is honest and straight forward. He may "jump to conclusions at times, but he'll learn to reason things out. It will come. He does a pretty good job now of using his head. He also has the kind of staying power it takes to open up this country and make something of it."

Chapter Two

Three days later Monty said to the ranch foreman, "Nathan, I'd like to ride into town for a short spell. That O.K.?" "Yes, just try to be back by supper, if you want any." OK", said Monty as he started for the corral. He saddled Blackjack and swung his leg over the saddle and started off at a good gallop. Blackjack was eager to run and stretched out his legs with ground eating strides. The brown that Monty had captured whinnied in protest that he didn't get to go. He ran a short distance along the fence that kept him homebound, he halfway reared in protest. The wind swept past Monty's hat with such force that caused him to shove the black flat rimed hat down on his head to keep from losing it. Blackjack was a picture to see. His tail nearly straight out, his head arched yet stretched forward and the wind blowing his mane. At his present pace he just seemed to glide across the prairie. And both horse and rider loved it.

When Monty rode into town he tied Blackjack in front of the sheriff's office. He opened the door and sheriff Baker looked up from his desk and then smiled as he said, "Boy, you didn't waste any time getting here, did you. I've got your money in the safe here." He got up and spun the dial on the safe a few times and opened it and pulled out a handful of money. "Eight hundred and fifty dollars. That's a lot of money for a cowboy. Someone rob a bank for you, Monty?" "No sir, he said, it's all nice and legal and it's a bit more than I expected. Sheriff, would you walk with me down to the Suds, I want a witness to what I'm about to do." "Sure." Monty turned and they walked down to the Suds. There were those same three cowboys sitting at the same table. They smiled as they saw Monty walk in. "Hey," said the slender cowboy," Here's the man that's going to beat Ole Jed's high priced race horse and win the county horse race." Monty grinned and tipped his hat to them. He looked at the Bartender and said, "I want to fill out one of those racing forms." The bartender reached under the bar and laid the form in front of Monty. He read it and then asked for a pencil and filled it out, then counted out five hundred dollars. "That should do it," said the bartender. "Not quite said Monty. I want a receipt." The bartender frowned and scribbled a receipt, mumbling under his breath. Monty then turned to the sheriff and said, "would you mind initialing this and dating it," asked Monty? The sheriff shook his head and muttered something under his breath and signed it. The three cowboys at the table snickered.

Then Monty asked Gabby, the bartender, "Are you the man holding the bets? "I am," he said. "What are the odds," asked Monty? Seven to one in favor of Jed," said the bartender. " Everybody knows about Jed's expensive horse but no one knows anything about that horse of yours. It could be that you just might change the stakes some," said the sheriff.

Monty then counted out three hundred and fifty dollars with another one hundred and fifty that he had saved. "Five hundred dollars on me," said Monty.

"It's your money, easy come, easy go, I guess. You want another receipt for that too?", asked the bartender sarcastically. "It's a good business practice." said Monty. "Sheriff Baker," said Monty as he slid the paper toward the sheriff. "what do you think the odds might be now that I've entered." asked Monty.

"Don't know, they might go up. You sure think a lot of that black horse of yours don't you?," said the sheriff. "He'll do," said Monty as he tipped his hat to the sheriff and turned and walked out the batwing doors. A smile crept across his lips. He hadn't told them he wouldn't be riding his black. He was going to ride his Brown stallion. There was nothing in the racing form that asked him what horse he was riding.

Monty rode into the ranch just at supper time. He unsaddled Blackjack and turned him loose in the corral and then walked up to the house. He went into the kitchen and sat down. Monte and the ranch hands had just finished eating.

Nathan looked at him and said, "Well, you going to keep us in suspense all night, what have you been up to?" Monty looked at each of them and then smiled as he said, " Now just what makes you think I've been up to something," he asked grinning. Nathan replied, "It's written all over your face kid. Come on, tell us."

"Well, I've just entered the county horse race." Rife Start, his chair leaning back against the wall, suddenly came down and with a look of surprise said, "Monty, have you ever seen Jed Bracket's horse run? He's the fastest thing I've ever seen, around here or anyplace else." "Well, Rife, you haven't seen my brown stallion when he was running all out, have you? He's got ground eating strides and a lot of wind. I'm not worried." "You mean your not riding Blackjack,? Asked Rife. "No," said Monte, I'm riding my brown stallion. The racing form didn't ask what horse I was riding, so no one knows but you fellers. I"de like to keep it that way."

Nathan said, "I've seen your Brown run but not all out. However, I have seen Jed's black run. I'd say this could be a mighty interesting race. Right now I think it's about a toss up, but I can tell you don't think so. You really do believe your stallion is going to win, don't you?" Monty avoided his question and said, " I'll need some time to prepare him. " "You got it," said Nathan. "Boy if you win, it sure will raise some eyebrows about this ranch, won't it? Another thing Monty, Blackjack is a lot easier to handle than that Stallion. Don't forget there's still some wildness in him. When Jed's horse sees that brown stallion of yours there may just be some trouble. You think your up to that?" Monty said he had given that some thought and he believed he could handle the Brown. He just hoped Jed could handle his horse. "Don't bet on it," said Rife.

The next day Monty saddled the Brown and rode off. He needed to get the Brown used to the idea of racing against other horses on a race track. He must win this race. This race wasn't just about winning. It was a race for his future.

His future with Beth. If he could win this race he would take his winnings and try to make a down payment on a ranch somewhere. Then he would begin to stock it. He had a plan working in his mind of just how he might do that.

The ground where he was now riding was fairly flat and level. He brought the Brown to a stop, waited for a couple of seconds, then kicked his heels to the Brown's flanks and yelled, 'Go, Brown, Go'" The Brown was totally surprised and bolted off to a jerky start, almost rearing. Monty rode him a short piece and reigned him in. He patted the brown's neck several times talking low as he patted his neck. After several minutes of this he repeated his start. After a few times the Brown was ready when Monty touched his boot to the flanks. After about an hour of this Monty let the Brown run all out. He could feel his horse's powerful muscles all working smoothly together. His back hind quarters propelled his powerful body forward and his forelegs reached out for distance. As Monty leaned forward on the stallion's neck, he spoke softly to him and patted his neck. The stallion was running as though this was what he was born to do, and as if he could do it forever. His life on the open range had prepared him for this. Monty reigned him in and walked him for a while. He then dismounted and took the horse's muzzle in his hand, again patted his neck, and the two walked together for about a mile. Monty then mounted and headed for the ranch. Just before supper he asked Zeke, Rife, and Nathan if they would help him. They said, "sure," and followed Monty to the corral. "I'd like for you to saddle your horses and line them up as if to race. I want my Brown to line up beside your mounts." They saddled up and lined up their horses and Monty put his Brown beside Nathan's buckskin gelding. Just then, Beth walked out the door and asked what was going on? Nathan explained they were trying to prepare the Brown for the upcoming race. "You want me to saddle up "Lady Luck" and join you, "she asked? "No," you take my pistol and fire it when your ready for us to start." She carefully took Nathan's colt and walked off several paces and held the gun in the air. "You ready," she asked? They nodded and she pulled the trigger.

    The Brown was much faster with his leap and was out in front in no time.

    They repeated this process a number of times, until Monty said he was satisfied and thanked all of them for their help.

    Nathan Frame knew something was going on in Monty's mind. This was more than just a race to him. He started to say something to Monty about it but decided to let it ride. If Monty wanted to talk about it he would in his own time and in his own way. Monty kept up his training of the Brown stallion.

    The day of the big race arrived. Folks came from all around to see which horse would take the prize money. The betting was pretty heavy and Jed Bracket's horse was picked as the favorite. Picnics were scattered all around the track with folks spreading their white tablecloths on the ground or wherever they found a favorable spot to enjoy a picnic of B B Q beef, fried chicken, potato salad and apple pie.. A band was playing, welcoming people to the grounds. A surprise event had just been announced. There was to be a wild horse riding contest , one hour after the big race. The prize was five hundred and fifty dollars to the winner. Monty went over and paid the entrance fee and then rode the Brown to the race track.

Suddenly there was another surprise. Monty and Beth heard a familiar voice yelling their names. They both turned in the direction of the voice and having their hopes dashed they tried to hide the frown within their hearts. They both forced a large grin on their faces. "Well, hello Vicky, they smiled. How nice to see you here." She answered, "oh, I wouldn't miss this race for anything. Especially, since you're riding in it, Nathan. You already win my vote as the best looking jockey riding today. I already have placed a bet on your horse to win." "Well, I hope you don't loose your money," said Monty. He took Beth's arm and started to maneuver her through the gathered crowd. Vicky called out to them, "Oh, don't leave me in this crowd. I want to sit with you." Monty looked at Beth and she shrugged her shoulders and they made room for her as they continued toward the bleachers. When they reach them they began pushing themselves upward until they reached the place they wanted. As they seated themselves, Monty kissed Bethany and said, "Wish me luck." As he turned to leave Vicky asked, "Don't you want my luck too? "Sure," said Monty as he again attempted to turn and leave. Vicky said, "Not that way," she said as she grabbed his arm and pulled him down and placed a kiss on his cheek. Monty's face turned red as he pulled himself away looking at Bethany. Vicky then turned to Bethany, smiled and said, "Oh, I hope he wins."

Horses were being gathered near the starting line. It was a three quarter mile race. Jed Bracket rode up to the inside lane. His black stallion was a sleek looking animal. He had good conformation and stout looking legs. Monte suspected there was some Morgan and Arabian breeding in his background. That was a good cross breeding for speed and endurance . But it also took good horse-handling to get the best out of him. Jed's horse tugged at his bit wanting to go. Jed was having trouble keeping him under control. He looked over and saw Monte riding the Brown. "That's not the horse your supposed to be riding, he shouted. Your supposed to be riding that black gelding. Monty answered back, "There's nothing in the racing form that said that," and he rode to the farthest outside lane. Jed's black stallion suddenly saw Monty's Brown stallion and reared high and issued a challenge to the brown stallion. The brown didn't flinch a bit. He, too reared up with ears laid back, and issued his own challenge. He was ready to meet Jed's black. Again the black reared and as he landed he bolted to meet Monty's brown. With ears laid back, their necks stretched out and their mouths open showing wicked looking teeth. The two stallions met, both riders were shouting trying to get their mounts under control. Other horses gathered for the race reacted in nervous jumps and crow hops. Both stallions reared high with their forelegs flailing and striking out. Then the black came down hard and kicked up his hind legs, unseating Jed. Immediately he made for the Brown. Monty was still seated on his Brown and was shouting and waving his hat at the approaching black. The two horses met and reared with their forelegs slashing. Monty was almost struck in the head. When the two horses came down the black ducked his head and with bared teeth reached for the Brown's left foreleg. The Brown, used to this kind of fighting, jerked his leg away and immediately spun around, almost unseating Monte, then he let loose with both hind feet catching the black on the shoulder with such force it knocked him side ways. Monty leaped from the saddle pulling the brown's reigns with him. Three other men grabbed the black and held him at bay. Jed's stallion shook his head and tried to rear up and as he did he favored his shoulder some. The men led him around a bit and there seemed to be no ill effects from the battle. They called for the vet and he examined Jed's black and decided that he was still fit to race. Jed was mad. He was yelling at the race officials about the brown attacking his horse and hurting his shoulder. He demanded that Monty Lane and his horse be disqualified. The officials reminded Jed that it was his horse that started the fight and pointed out that had others not interfered Monty's stallion would have done more damage.

Jed was furious. He looked at his dad and demanded he do something. His dad walked over to the officials and tried to get them to disqualify Monte and his Brown but the judges were firm in their decision. Stew Bracket then walked back out to Jed and just shrugged his shoulders indicating there was nothing more he could do. He told Jed to give a good ride. Jed jerked the black's reins and led him back to the starting line. Monty calmed down the Brown and got him positioned. All the horses were brought to the starting line. Beth was so nervous, she couldn't set still. She yelled to Monty, "Good luck, Monty!" She wasn't aware that she was biting her lip so, until she realized the pain. As she checked to see if it was bleeding, Vicki's voice rose loudly, "Good luck, Monty, you handsome brute." Beth was so embarrassed she put her racing schedule up to her face. Vicki noticed and only grinned.

Jed's Black was mouthing his bit nervously. A palomino snorted stretching his neck up and down. A mouse colored gelding nervously shuffled his feet. Monty had the Brown poised and ready. After a couple of anxious moments the official pointed his pistol toward the heavens and fired. They were off. The black leaped into the lead, pulling away in several lengths. A red gelding was a strong second. A paint and the mouse colored dun were moving up on the red. They passed the one quarter mark and Monty was letting the brown get the feel of the track not pushing him at all. The fans in the stands were yelling for their favorite horse, the Black, to run faster. Beth stood with her hands clasped together at her chest not saying a word. Vicki, on the other hand was standing yelling as loud as she could, "Go Monty, Go. Go faster." Nathan and the ranch hands were all yelling their support for Monty. Vicky was yelling for Monty to "go," "go", "go." As they reached the half way mark the Brown began to pull at his bit wanting to go faster. Monty gave a little slack to his reins but not enough for the brown to get it in his teeth. The Brown pulled along side of the golden palomino. He was a beautiful horse to watch. His color glistened in the bright sun. After a few strides Monty urged his Brown stallion to move up to where three horses were bunched close together. As Monty urged the Brown for more speed he had it to give. His running so fast was not punishment as some folks thought. No, the Brown loved to run and he was running. Yet, he was still holding back, waiting for his Master to let him run top speed. The black was about five lengths into the lead. Monty moved up beside the bunched horses and stayed there several strides then called on the brown who responded with that powerful stride of his. After about five more strides Monty again urged the Brown to move ahead. The Brown was game. It was as if he was back on the prairie again running with his mares. Without breathing hard the Brown increased his speed. His legs seemed to stretch out even farther. His hooves pounded the hard surface of the track with an even rhythm, His mane was blowing in the wind and his head was stretched forward as if wanting to go even faster. For his own reasons Monte did not want the Brown Stallion's true speed to be known. Not yet anyway. Monte eased his stallion past the bunched horses and began to close in on the black stallion that had attacked him. He leaned forward as much as he dared and began encouraging the brown to run faster still. Monte was stretching the brown lengthening his strides, on the black stallion, as if getting revenge. As they pushed down the home stretch the brown had moved along side the black. In just a few seconds they were neck and neck. The crowd in the stands were all on their feet, yelling and cheering. Jed raised his whip to the black, but the black had already given his best. He had been pushed too hard, too fast, too long. His hard running had been limited to track running.

Monty's Brown had run at hard speeds for miles escaping from the dangers of the plains and the steep hills. He had mastered those hills surrounding the plains where he was born, building strong muscles. Again Jed raised his whip only this time he swung it toward Monty. The sharp ends stung Monty on the face. The crowd shouted their disapproval of Jed's action. Again he raised the whip but this time as he brought it down, Monty reached out and grabbed it, and pulled it away from him. Then he threw it on the track. Monty leaned forward and patted the brown's neck for they were coming down to the finish line. Monty was leaning forward patting the brown's neck, talking to him, urging the great stallion for more speed and he had it to give. He shot past the fading black and crossed the finish line six lengths ahead. The crowd went wild, jumping up and down, throwing Stetsons into the air, hugging one another, running to meet the winner in the winner's circle. Of course there were those who wore a big frown because of the money they had lost betting on Jed's black stallion. It was the first time he had ever been beaten. Monty walked his stallion toward the winner's circle. The Brown stood proud in the circle, his ears perked forward. His mouth was chewing at the bit. Ever few minutes he would raise his head up and down, and then shake it from side to side. He would move smoothly from side to side in the winners circle.

Monty swung out of the saddle and held the Brown still while others admired him at a distance. He was a picture to behold, as he stood erect, his face focused straight ahead, his ears pointed straight up, his eyes looking straight ahead. He was indeed a beautiful animal. One man approached Monty, offering him ten thousand dollars for the stallion. Monty said the Brown was not for sale at any price. Another man came and offered five hundred to breed his mare to the Brown. Again Monty rejected the offer. Then the man doubled his offer. Monty shook his head "no." saying he was going to build his own herd with this stallion. No one heard Monte's remark except Nathan Frame, foreman of the Circle B. He sort of grinned and kept it to himself. Things were beginning to add up. Things he approved of. Thirty-five hundred dollars from his wager plus three thousand winnings. That was more money than Monty Lane had ever seen in his life. The Circle B crew crowded around Monty congratulating him on his winnings. Nathan and three of the Circle B held up their hands with wads of money for they too had won on the Brown. Beth put her arms around him and gave him a long and hard hug. Even when Monty had relaxed his arms around her she continued to squeeze. Then she turned her lips toward his and kissed him. Then with a wide grin she asked, "Is that enough money to marry me,"?

Not knowing how to respond, Monty stepped back and turned toward the Brown pretending to calm him down. She had aroused feelings in him that he hadn't known before and it frightened him. Then two arms went around him and a voice said, "Oh, Monty, I'm so proud of you. You deserve a kiss and a hug." With that Vicky reached up and placed an arm around his neck and pulled him down to her and placed her lips firmly on his and pulled her body up closer to his and then still even closer to his. Monty reached out his hands and took her by her elbows and pushed her down and away. He said to her, "Ma'am, I'm not yours to be held that way. She smiled at him and said, "oh, I'm sorry Monty, I never dreamed you wouldn't enjoy it." "I certainly did." … "Anytime, Monty, anytime."

With that she backed off, not looking at Beth , who was embarrassed, angry, and surprised. She looked at Vicky and said, "Vicky, please don't do that again. Monty's mine. I don't intend to share him. You and I have been friends for a long time. Please don't spoil it with such foolishness. Nathan is in love with me not you. He's embarrassed by your advances."

Vicky looked at Beth and said, "I'm sorry Beth. I don't deliberately want to hurt you. We have been friends for a long time. But Beth, if I can win his love, I'm going to…friends or no friends. I'm sorry." She turned and walked away.

As Vicky walked away Bethany put both hands on her hips and said, "Vicky, I I haven't begun to fight… yet."

Monty quickly scooted over by Beth and took hold of her hand. Beth placed her arm around Monty indicating that he belonged to her. Vicky only smiled at both.

Gabby showed up and gave him his sixty five hundred dollars. "Son, no one knew that horse of yours and you turned the spread a little wider. You sure rode one heck of a ride. Here's your money." Monty couldn't believe his good fortune.

Chapter Three

Sitting on his horse, off at a distance, Jed Bracket cursed Monty Lane under his breath. He was supposed to win this race. He was supposed to be in the winners circle, showing off this new black horse his daddy had bought him. And Beth, she was supposed to be hugging him. Not Monty Lane! Well, Monty Lane wasn't going to get away with this. He would find a way to get even. Then suddenly he thought of a way. He uttered under his breath, "Monty Lane, I hate you. You hear that Monty Lane, I hate you and some day I will get even with you. Yes, sir, I will get even with you, and I will have Beth, too!" Then he rode off looking for two men in particular, Jess Parker and Lot Stringer. They were the town ruffians who liked to bully people. They had been involved in numerous saloon fights and they were for hire. They had worked for Jed before. Once he had them to beat up a fellow because he had gone calling on a girl Jed was sweet on. When he found his town ruffians he asked them if they wanted to make five hundred dollars each. They asked what they had to do, like it mattered. "Does it matter," he asked? "No," they grinned. "We've worked for you before. You always pay well." What do you want us to do." "I want you to keep your eye on that Hale "feller" and when he starts for home I want you ambush him and take his money and then shoot that brown stallion of his," he said. "What about the cowboy?" "No, don't shoot him unless you have to. I want to see him without that cursed horse of his. I'll handle him myself, said Jed. "We'll need more men than just us," said Jess. "All right, get Will Gordon, Dan Holt, and Neeley Pearce. Tell them I'll give them three hundred each. Don't tell them how much your getting." They both grinned at Jed, nodded approval and left.

Suddenly Monty's thoughts were interrupted by the blaring announcement that the bucking broncho contest was about to begin. He hurried over to the window and paid his entrance fee. He drew number fourteen, Twisting Cyclone. Just his luck.

That horse was reported to be unridable. Monte commented to Nathan his luck of the draw. Nathan replied, "Don't sweat about it Monte. Remember there's never been a horse that couldn't be ridden." Monte answered back, "Yeah, and there's never been a rider than can't be thrown." Nathan chucked and said, "Oh, you heard that too?" "Unfortunately yes," said Monte.

Seven riders rode before Monty. Two of them had ridden their mounts to the time line. It was now Monty's turn. He went to the chute. The horse was readied and ready for him. The Chestnut leaped against the side of the chute when Monty tried to climb down on him. Finally, they got him settled down enough for Monty to get both legs into position and slipped them into the stirrups. He grabbed the rope pulled back on it and yelled, "let'er go." And go he did! Twister bolted from his chute with his head down and all four feet off the ground. He did three high crow hops squealing with each one. He came down hard with his front feet pounding hard and his back feet kicking straight back. Then he reared straight up, his forelegs striking at an imaginary enemy and walked two steps. Monty leaned forward keeping his balance ready for a fishtail or for his head to jerk down. The crowd was wild, on their feet yelling words of encouragement to him. The whole Circle B crew were rooting for him. Monty was concentrating on his ride but still heard shouts like, "Stay with him Monty." "Hang in there cowboy." He was sure trying. He managed to keep his one arm swinging in the air as the horse spun to the right and then the left. Monty felt his insides being shook violently. Yet he managed to hang on and rub his heels against the bronc's flanks. This of course only made the horse to buck more violently. But the judges liked it. Suddenly the bronc whirled completely around and landed all four feet flat and savagely swung his head down to the left and kicked his heals again toward the right. Monty did not feel his hat fall off, but felt daylight between himself and the horse as he slid off balance momentarily. He managed somehow to hang on and prepare himself for another twisting whirl when the buzzer sounded and a rider was there to help Monty to unload himself from the Twister. The crowd went wild and cheered Monty for he had given a good ride. He took his hat from one of the riders and waved it at them. They cheered again some of them standing to their feet. Twister had just been ridden. Beth, Nathan, and the Circle B Riders were there to congratulate Monty. Again Beth encircled her arms around him and this time kissed him on the cheek. Monty's cheeks reddened from embarrassment. As the crowd began to settle down, a woman's voice rang out above the crowd's, "Monty, dear, I love you!" Monty looked at Beth and said, "Do you think that woman will ever give up?" Beth smiled at him and said, "I don't care, as long as you love me. That's what counts." With that they squeezed one another's hand.

Twenty minutes later they announced the winner of the bronc riding contest.. The announcer stated that there were three riders who had ridden to the buzzer and their scores were very close but the judges unanimously agreed that the best ride was given by Monty Lane of the Circle B Ranch. Again the crowd applauded their approval. Monty walked out and again waved his hat to the crowd and then went over and collected his One hundred fifty dollars. It was that much more for his dream. But sitting in the crowd were two who were not cheering. Rather Jed and his dad's face had no sign of pleasantness about them at all. While his dad's face was full of disapproval of Monte's victory, Jed's eyes were filled with hate and his face was cold sober. Under his breath he uttered, "One of these days Lane you will get your due. One of these days." He then got up and left. His dad followed.

Nathan turned to Beth and said, "Boy, winning the county race and the bronc riding contest-all in the same day. The Circle B is coming up in the world".

Nathan, Rife, and Beth had started for the Circle B while Monty was getting his winnings. Monty and Zeke hung around for a few minutes then they too started toward the ranch. Zeke was asking Monte about the race and especially riding that bronc. "Boy," he said, "That was sure some ride. Yes Sir, it was at that." They were about three miles out of town when all of sudden five gunmen came riding out of the brush not twenty feet away. Monty and Zeke pulled their horses to an abrupt halt. All five were masked and held their guns on them. "All right, put those hands up and nobody will get hurt." "You," pointing to Monty, "Toss those saddle bags over here." At that moment Monty's Brown Stallion violently shook his head and let out a stallion challenge and lunged at one of the would be robber's horse, which also was a stallion. The thief's stallion jumped to one side. The two closest outlaws, Jess Parker and Lot Stringer took their eyes off of Monty to glance at The Brown. When they looked back at Monty and Zeke, Monty's gun was in his hand. He fired and Jess Parker grabbed his middle and then fell out of the saddle. The second man, Lot Stringer, started to swing his gun toward Monty and Monty fired a second time. Stringer too fell to the ground. The third would be thief said, "Lets get out of here and they all three turned their horses and spurred away. Monty and Zeke didn't give chase. Instead Monty dismounted and looked at each man. There was nothing to be done for either of them. "You know them Zeke," asked Monty. "Yeah, I know them. They never were up to any good." He leaned forward with both hands on the pommel and said, "I've heard they did some work for Jed Bracket, but noone's been able to prove anything on them." Monty picked up the would be robbers guns and then searched their pockets. He found a few dollars. Then he collected their horses. He went through their saddle bags and found a little over three hundred dollars in each one. "That's interesting," said Zeke. "Isn't it though," said Monty. "Seems to me that, dead, I must worth about a thousand dollars to someone, considering those who rode away were paid about the same. Someone sure must want me dead awful bad." "You don't think it was just robbery," asked Zeek? "No, I don't. I believe Jed Bracket is behind this but I have no proof. He want's me out of the picture and I suspect it's more than just a horse race." "Why's that," asked Zeke? "Let's just say I've got a hunch," said Monty, "I've got a hunch."

They laid the two would be robbers across their horses and started back to town for the sheriff's office. Monty didn't know this new appointed sheriff very well. It seems that Sheriff Dillard resigned and left town. He gave no warning or reason. He just turned in his badge and left. The Mayor and the town council had hired a new sheriff, Ben Baker. As they pulled their mounts up in front of the sheriff's office , he was just coming out the door. "What's this?, what's happened?" He asked. Monty told him about the attempted robbery. They both shot in self defense. He looked at Monty and said, "Boy, they told me trouble just seemed to follow you around and it looks like it does at that." Monty looked into the eyes of the sheriff and said, "I don't go hunting trouble sheriff, but I don't run from it either." The Sheriff raised the head of each dead man and then looked at Zeke. "What happened Zeke? Monty put in, "What's the matter sheriff, don't you believe I told you the truth?" Angrily the sheriff pointed his finger at Monty and said, "I've heard your story Lane, and now I just want to hear Zeke's. I'm not insinuating anything. So just shut up and let me listen! You understand?" The new sheriff was near forty and built just a little lighter than Monty, but he was a solidly built man. His shoulders were wide, his arms long, and his middle thin. He had black hair and high cheek bones. He stood up to Monty like a man with bark on. Monty bristled but remained quiet. Zeke began to give the same details of the attempted robbery. When he finished, the sheriff turned and looked at Monty from his guns to his face and said, "You're mighty quick with those guns aren't you Lane" Monty again bristled and replied, "They had us covered Sheriff. Would you rather I let him shoot us? Or maybe you think I should have just handed over my hard earned winnings to them. If you mean I drew faster than they could shoot, that I admit." The sheriff turned to Zeek and said, "One of these days he's going to be too fast, and he going to be in trouble." Monty started to answer but Zeke held up his hand to Monty and said to the sheriff, "What happens to all that cash they had on them." "Probably goes to the county," said the sheriff. Monty started again to say something but Zeke looked at him and gave him a firm look and said, "No Monty, leave it alone." With that he turned his horse and started out of town. Monty muttered something under his breath and followed Zeke. The sheriff yelled at them to come back, but they continued toward the ranch. Monty turned in his saddle and yelled back to the sheriff, "I'll be back in town tomorrow." He looked at Zeke and said, "You know what? I"m beginning to think that new sheriff doesn't like me. I really don't understand why, I've never done anything to him."

Zeek shook his head a couple of times but said nothing.

When Monty and Zeek got home they told Nathan about the attempted robbery.

Zeke added, "Nathan, you should have been there and seen Monty in action. Man I thought we were dead ducks. I was right beside Monty and I didn't even see him draw. But then there was a gun in his hand blasting away at those robbers. He shot both of those thieves before they knew what hit them. Boy, it sure was a good thing your brown acted up at just the right moment." "He didn't do it without prompting," Monty said. I touched him in the flanks." "That was quick thinking" said Nathan. Monty just shrugged. "You do handle those guns pretty well, don't you." "With some anger in his voice he turned to Nathan and said, "You got something to say Nathan?" "No," said Nathan. "You were justified in what you did. It's just I don't want you to develop a bad reputation. You know, this news is going to travel around about how good you are with those guns and somewhere there's going to be somebody who is going

In Pursuit of a Dream | 25

to come and try you. Probably more than one." "I know," Nathan said, "but I don't know what to do about it. Nathan, I don't want to kill people, but it seems like I'm left no choice. I've thought about changing my name and going someplace else like Nevada or California." "Well, let's hope it doesn't come to that," said Nathan. "No matter where you go and how far you travel, it seems the past always has a way of catching up with you."

"A man does have a right to defend himself Monty, but chew on the fact that often violence breeds violence. We live in tough times, Monty, but there's coming a time when matters will have to be settled differently between people. That's why we have laws and courts. One of these days, in your lifetime, and mine, we're going to see it. When this does happen, Monty, if you don't change with it your going to have to suffer the consequences." Monty looked at Nathan and said, "Gosh, Nathan, you sound like a preacher or a judge." Nathan grinned and said, "Well, I don't mean to be. But a better system of Law and order is just a coming fact."

Chapter Four

The next morning found Monty Lane in town in a lawyers office, He hired him to do all the legwork in paying the back taxes on Baldy Briggs's ranch that Ron Arthus had stolen from him. (Book 1) . After he had been killed and Arthus jailed, the whole matter of his ranch had been sort of put on hold. No kin of Briggs had been found so everything was sort of in limbo, even though a search had been made and advertised in several news papers. Monty found that Briggs owed $3000 in back taxes and Arthus had never paid it. He just made it look like he had in the bank ledgers. Monty instructed the lawyer to draw up the papers and be his go-between in purchasing the ranch. Once the ranch was in his name he was to see if there any other bills that were held against the ranch and to pay them. He was to borrow three thousand dollars against his ranch. No one was to know who the real purchaser was until he was ready for the public to know.

It was time that Monty went to see the new Sheriff and have a talk with him.

As he rode to the sheriff's office he was surprised to see Jed Bracket there. "There he is, Sheriff, arrest him. Arrest him right now and put him in Jail," yelled Jed. Monty looked surprised then felt anger begin to swell up within him. "Arrest me for what," asked Monty. "For killing my two friends, Jess Parker and Lot Stringer. You murdered them in cold blood." Monty suddenly backhanded Jed without any warning. Jed fell back against the wall. "Why you," said Jed as he reached for his gun but suddenly let go of it when he saw Monty's gun already in his hand, It was pointed at Jed's middle, and the hammer was back. Sheriff Baker told Monty to put his gun away and for Jed to simmer down and to shut up. "Now then, let's see if we can solve this without any more violence." Monte flipped his colt into his holster and said, "Sheriff, what has this idiot been telling you about me?" "Well, he said these five friends of his stopped you on the way home, just out of town, and started arguing with you, accusing you of cheating in that race. Then, he says, that you just up and shot them. No reason, just shot them.

How would he know what happened. I didn't see him anywhere near. "That's because I was hid in the trees," said Jed. Suddenly he realized that he had just incriminated himself. "Well, Well, it's beginning to become quite clear to me now," said Monty. "You put those men up to that because I beat you in that race. You little weasel, you don't have the guts to do your own dirty work so you hire someone to do it for you. I found over four hundred dollars on both those scum you hired. Was that all of it or were you going to give them a bonus when I was dead?" "All right, this has gone far enough," said the sheriff. " Monty, do you have anyone to back up your story?" asked the Sherif. Monte quickly brought his temper under control suspecting what the sheriff was trying to do. "You bet I do," Sheriff. One of the Circle B riders, Zeke Gage, was riding with me. He can tell you everything that happened. "All right, I'll ride out and talk to him," said the Sheriff." "But sheriff, these two guys work together. Their friends, you can't trust what he says," said Jed. Then the sheriff turned to Jed and said, "Now, Jed, you just told us you were there and just maybe you had a lot more to do with what happened than your telling. So go home and stop trying to stir up trouble. I mean that Jed or I'll toss your hide in jail. You got that? It's pretty clear to me what really happened. I just can't prove it….yet. But I will tell your daddy about what you just did." Jed was so angry he could hardly keep his voice down, but he looked at the Sheriff and said, "I'm going home all right. I'm going home and tell my daddy how you took this saddle tramp's side and let a murderer run loose. Daddy will see to it that your no longer Sheriff in this town." "Well, I think you've already told me that and if this badge doesn't mean any more than that, he can have it," said Sheriff Baker. Jed bolted out of the jail and quickly mounted his horse and sped down the main street with his black running all out. Two men had to jump out of the way to keep from being knocked down. Both men turned and shook their fist at Jed.

"Am I free to go Sheriff," asked Monty. "Yeah, for now." Monty took a couple of steps and then turned around and looked at the sheriff. "Sheriff, I guess I got off on the wrong foot with you and I'm sorry. I'd like nothing more than for you and I to be friends." Sheriff Baker extended his hand and said, "I'd like that, too, Monty. They shook hands and then the sheriff indicated a chair and said, "Why not pull up a chair and set a spell." Monty sat down and the sheriff said, "Monty, I'm sorry I had to put you through all that awhile ago with Jed. But I wanted him to face up to all that you and Zeke had told me. We caught him in a lie and now he knows I know he was involved. Even though I can't prove it…yet. But I will tell his dad that he needs to take better care of Jed. Some day Jed is going to make a bad mistake and he will have to answer for it. And his daddy won't be able to bail him out of it." Monte stayed with the sheriff for over an hour. When he left he felt he had made a friend. Outside the ranch Monte felt he had no friends,,.except maybe the sheriff. Other than that he felt he could trust no one. Monty mounted his Brown and started for the Circle B. On the way home he was thinking of a new adventure. He now had a ranch, but only two horses. He didn't want a cattle ranch. Beth had a good cattle ranch. He wanted a horse ranch. And he knew how to get a good start. It would take a lot of hard work and it would be risky but he was no stranger to that. He would need to rebuild the bunk house but the house and barn were solidly built. Except where he had dynamited it. (See previous book- "The Blurred Hand")

It wouldn't be as large as Beth's ranch but it would be a lot more than he owned right now.

First he needed more cash. And he had plans on how to get it. He thought about the brakes along the river that ran through Beth's ranch and his newly acquired ranch and all the brush that held more wild cattle than a dog has fleas in the middle of dog town. He had seen some of those cows as he rode the range looking for strays. If he could round them up and buy some more he could do a cattle drive to Abilene.

He had been on trail drives before and he knew some of the ins and outs about them. But he had never been a trail boss, but he had been a ramrod. He had worked for two good trail bosses and learned a lot from them.

Now take that Bill Hyatt down in south west Texas. That man had a lot of savvy when it came to driving cows. He was always planning his next move. He always thought about the "what ifs" and when they happened, he just seemed to be ready. Sure, they had stampedes but he learned how to work with them and not let it get the best of his crew. He also had a lot of bark on him.

He fought against herd cutters, indians, drought and bad weather. Bill Hyatt never " back peddled" from anyone. Yes sir, he had learned a lot from old Bill. He also was a patient man and a fair man with his crew. Monty had made mistakes and learned some hard lessons with Bill Hyatt. Now if he could round up a thousand head of those "onery" cows in the brakes, buy a thousand more at $5 a head and sell them at a good price he would be able to stock his ranch. And one thing Texas had right now was cattle. Lots and lots of cattle and lots of land, but no money. Texas was broke. And the east was hungry for Texas beef.

The Texas plains had all kinds of wild horse herds running loose right now. And there were some great horses mixed in those herds. They would make great mounts when captured and gentled.

A month later, Monty rode into Ludwig and stopped at the Suds. He ordered a glass of beer. The bartender, Gabby, said to him, ""Monty, when you come in here you always order a glass of beer, and you never drink it. What's with you, anyway."

Monty grinned and said, "I don't know, maybe I just want to bounce things off you and pay you for your time so I'll feel better." "I need to hire some good cowhands for a trail drive." "Trail drive? Where you going to get enough cattle for a trail drive, or is this for the Circle B. "No, Gabby, this is strictly for me. And don't worry, I'll get the cattle." "Boy, you can lose both your life and your shirt on one of those things. You ever been on a trail drive before?" " Yes Gabby I have, and I've given this a lot of thought. It's something I am determined to do. But I need to hire some good hands first, got any suggestions?" "Good suggestion Gabby, not just any cowhand. Gabby looked down at the bar and then back at Monty. "Well, lets see," Gabby was wondering out loud, "There's Tom Wells and Shorty Briggs of the Triple Slash. They were in yesterday and they said they were being let go at the end of the month because their boss couldn't afford them any more until spring. They're good men too. Then, I remember that Curly Springs, Lefty Gates, and Mack Shears over at the Circle H. They've got the same problem," said Gabby. Say, how about those three cowboys sitting over there, asked Monty. Are they worth hiring? "I wouldn't hire them to throw out dishwater" said Gabby in disgust. " They're worthless."

"Say now, ole Sam Meyers has two sons that just came home from the war and their looking for work. Their names are Sam and Sidney." Their good boys, too." That Sam now he can ride about anything with hair. And Sidney, he's mighty good with a gun. Long gun or short. And he hits what he aiming at, too. I hear it said he was a scout for the army."

"Thanks Gabby, I owe you big time. "Good luck," said Gabby as Monty turned and left. Monty rode to the Circle H and then the Triple Slash. First he talked to the owners and then the men the bartender had named. All were anxious to sign up.

At the Triple Slash Monty also picked up another hand by the name of Red Barter, a tall good looking Texan with a lot of red hair. He was a good hand with horses and cattle. He was also a man who would fight for the brand. Well, now that the word was out he just might pick up a few more. Monty rode back to the Circle B, Nathan came to the corral and as Monty was dismounting Nathan said, "I thought you got lost." Monty first told him of his going to see the sheriff and their trying to start over again. He told Nathan, "You know I like that sheriff. I never had any close friends before, except you, and the crew here. It feels good." Then he told him of his trail drive plans, and what he had been doing.

Nathan said he thought Monty had a solid idea but a trail drive was a hard and dangerous job and bossing a crew was even harder. The two talked for over an hour about it. Nathan had been over the trail himself and had even "bossed" one for Beth's dad. He told Monty he would draw him a map with the streams and rivers on it. He also suggested that Monty take 500 of Beth's cattle and sell them for Beth. If he did that he could let Shorty and Justin Banks go with him. That would help lessen the load for him and the crew while he was gone. And the sale of 500 cattle would be good for Beth's bank account… although it was doing fine.

He would hire a new crew while they were gone. Monty thanked him and then walked up to the big house and knocked on the door. Beth came and asked him in. He removed his hat and said, "Beth, I've got something to say to you and don't stop me until I've finished, O.K.?"

She nodded with a puzzled look on her face. Monty took a breath and swallowed kind of hard and began. "Beth, first let's sit down. I feel kind of weak in my knees… Remember, I love you and I very much want you for my wife. First there was a bewildered look on Beth's face…then tears suddenly appeared in her eyes and started to spill from her eyes down her cheeks.. There was a hint of a smile forming with her lips. Monty suddenly knew this was not good. But he had already started so he might as well continue. Beth, I have nothing to offer you right now, but I will have. And not too long from now. I just can't marry you for your ranch." She rolled her eyes as if to say, "Here we go again."

Monty continued, "Beth, I'm planning on gathering a lot of cattle from those brakes on the ranch along the river and then I'm going to buy enough to make a herd of about two thousand head and trail them to Abilene. I've already talked with Nathan and he thinks it's a good idea and suggested I take 500 of your cattle and sell them as well. When I return I'll have enough money to ask you to marry me." She was silent for a minute, then asked, "Monty, why are you doing this? It's so dangerous. Monty, how can I convince you that what I want is you? Not what you can give me. I already have all I want. All except you, Monty Lane. You're all I want, I don't need anything else."

"But, Beth, don't you see, when this is done I will have something to offer you, I'm really doing this for us." "But you don't have too!" she protested. "Yes, Bethany, I do. It's the only way I can. I figure we'll be gone between two or three months at the most and maybe less than a month to get back. Then we'll have the rest of our lives together… And I'll be able to start that horse ranch"

"Does it mean that much to you, Monty? She asked? "Yes, Beth, it does. I will be able to hold my head high without any kind of guilt, no matter who I meet or where I go." "Beth, looked down for a couple of seconds then raised her head and said, "well I don't feel I have any choice, Monty." "I love you, no matter what…I'll be waiting for you when you get back. And I will entrust you into God's hands. And I will pray that you're dream will come true. I'll pray every day that God will keep you safe." "Don't forget the crew, " said Monty. "I won't, Monty. And I'll not be at peace about this until you and the hands return." Monty and Beth stood up and hugged. Then Beth and Monty went outside. As he started to walk away it suddenly dawned upon him he still hadn't asked Beth to marry him. He had only told Beth his plans. He didn't ask her to marry him, he just sort of took it for granted that she would. He turned around and went back and knocked on the door. When she opened the door he sheepishly grinned and said, "That is if you will still have me. Beth, Will you marry me? I promise I will try hard to make you a good husband. I've wanted you for my wife from the first moment I saw you." Beth giggled and put her arms around his neck and kissed him. "Of course I'll marry you, Monty Lane, but you can be a mighty stubborn man sometimes. But I love you in spite of it." He grinned and said, "I guess it's just part of my charm," And he held her close and kissed her again. Suddenly he felt strange feelings welling up in him. Feelings that made him feel like he never wanted to leave or let her go. He took his arms from around her and she grinned at him. He said he better go and stepped back from her and headed for the pasture where Blackjack was kept. As he approached the gelding the horse whinnied and started walking toward him. Monty was so anxious to tell somebody the good news, and his horse was the first he saw. He had to go and tell Blackjack the news.

He never told Beth about his ranch. That would be the biggest surprise of all.

The next time Monty talked to Nathan about the drive Nathan told him about a trail cook he knew and he had his own wagon. He also was savvy about trail drives and would be a big help to him. That sounded good to Monty. He also decided to take another wagon to carry more supplies. As Monty rode the range checking the Circle B stock he kept thinking about the trail drive and began to make plans for it. He made a list of the supplies he would need. Several weeks later the trail cook that Nathan mentioned showed up. The first person he saw was Nathan walking toward the "big house." The driver halted his team of mules , got down from the wagon and approached Nathan. "Howdy", said the driver. Nathan stopped and with a friendly smile said, "Howdy, can I help you?" "I hope so. Are you Mister Nathan?" "Well, the last time I heard, that's what people called me," answered Nathan. "I understand your looking for a good trail cook."

Nathan pointed to Monty at the corral working with a new horse. He said, "He does." The cook walked over to Monty who was bent over pulling at a saddle. The cook tapped Monty on the shoulder. "You the "feller" looking for a trail cook? When Monty looked up the cook said, "Say, you look awful young to boss a trail drive, how old are you ?" "Do you shave yet?"

Monty stared at the cook in surprise. Then he said, " I'm old enough to do the job." The cooked backed up a step and said, "You looked at me with surprise, what's the matter, Mr. Nathan not tell you I am black?" "No, he didn't and that doesn't matter to me at all. I do remember that he recommend you very highly though, both as a cook and the savvy for trail drives", said Monty. "I've done my share," he said. "What's your name?" asked Nathan. He reached up to scratch his partially bald grey head and said, "Well, now, I Don't rightly remember. Folks call me "Short Bread" so long, that's all I ever known." The two men talked about the drive and the supplies a cook would need." Monty told him about his idea to buy another wagon to haul some supplies that 'Shortbread's' wagon wouldn't hold. Shortbread thought that was a good idea and handed him a list of supplies he would need for the trail. Monte asked Nathan if Short Bread could bunk with them in the bunkhouse until they left for the drive. Nathan replied, "No problem." The next day Nathan went with Monty to find some of the supplies they needed. They rode into Ludwig. They went to several stores, a black smith shop, and a stable. Then there was a general store and a gun smith shop. At the far end of town there was a wagon yard and mules loose in the corral. They talked to the holster there who kept an ear out for such things. He gave them a few suggestions of where to look for what. After looking around Monty bought a wagon, mules and harness. They haggled a bit about the price but finally each side compromised and the deal was made. Then the two of them went to the general store and started ordering the supplies he would need for the long trail. Nathan was able to make some good suggestions and Monte listened to him. He also bought a thousand rounds of ammunition, The store keep asked, "You going to start a war?" "No, just finish one if it starts." "Oh, two tarps, two extra wagon wheels, axil grease, tar for the wagon cracks, bailing wire, axes, salve for cuts, water barrels and other items Shortbread and Nathan thought they would need. Shortbread would order the food and store what he could in his wagon. As careful as Monte was about his money, he saw it was beginning to disappear. In two more weeks all the crew had arrived. There was Tom Wells and Shorty Brigs of the Slash Three, Curley Springs, Mack Shorn, and Lefty Gates from the Circle H, the two brothers, Mark and Sidney Meyers and Red Barter. Nathan had also promised to loan him Zeek Gage and Rife Stout for the drive since he was taking 500 of the Circle B cows.

Their first big job was rounding up the cows in the brakes and branding them.

Monte met with his crew and talked about his reason for this drive. He told them this was his first trail drive as boss. He would be open for suggestions but his word would be final. If they had any doubts about his ability, then now was the time to say it. He also told them about their having a black cook. If they had any problems with that, now would be the time to leave. No one voiced any opposition. In the West a man made his own way. He was what he was and no one questioned about his past. Especially after they were told he was a good cook. On a trail drive, that went a long way, understanding and patience covered a multitude of sins. Once they had all signed on, they were told they had signed on for the long haul. They would finish the drive. There would be no quitting. If any man quit he forfeited the money he had earned. If they finished with a good job under his belt they got a week's bonus.

Monty said he would tolerate no drinking on the drive. They could play cards but no gambling. He looked at each man and waited for their response. They readily agreed. You understand then that you will complete the drive and live up to my instructions. Again they voiced a "yes." He directed to the back of a wagon and told them to sign their name or make their mark on the paper in the back of the wagon.

The next day they all rode with Monty to the river brakes. The grass was good and plentiful, but those brakes were filled with briars, tangled vines, thorn bushes, Mesquite bushes and rattlers. It was like God took all the bad stuff he had left over after the Creation and dumped it along the rivers. And the cows were some of the meanest, the orneriest, and most cantankerous critters on this side of Hell. They would be wild and some of them wicked with razor sharp horns. Some of those steers would be nearly as tall as a horse with horns close to five feet wide. Many a rider had lost his life because of such mavericks. At times they would hide from a rider and when he appeared then it would rush him and his horse. If the rider fell off he was often a dead man. And many a good horse had been gored by them. As they rounded up the cattle they would bunch them as a herd and then drive them toward Monty's new ranch and brand them there, another hot and tough job.

Parts of Monty's ranch wasn't that far from the brakes. The cattle would stay at the ranch because there was plenty of grass and water. Monty posted two men to watch them at all times. They would rotate this job among his crew.

Then the fun began. At first it was easy, there were so many cattle in the brakes. They would find ten to fifteen together in a clearing and start them toward the make-shift cattle pen. Once they found nearly fifty near a water hole. But they were wild and did not go willingly. They would dart off into the brush and had to be roped and hauled out. They continued to round up three hundred more and drove them over to his ranch and started branding them. They had a number of cows and calves mixed in with the steers. They branded them all but would leave the calves behind. They would stay there with some of the older cows where there was plenty of food and shelter. Monty's brand was The M/B. Obviously it stood for Monty and Beth. When he returned they would be wed. Then the gathering began to get harder. Those cows knew they were being hunted and they didn't want to be found. There were some mean ones in that brush too. One ole brindle steer had horns that were nearly five feet from tip to tip and razor sharp . When pushed they would sometimes charge at the riders. When this happened Monty and Short both put ropes on it, they then drug it out into the open and Short roped its hind legs. When their horses stretched him out, he went down and Monty leaped from Blackjack and quickly "hogtied" it. The steer would thrash and bawl until it wore itself out .Then one of the riders would return and turn it loose. It was a lot easier to manage after that.

One day as they were beating the brush for cows, a big old black and white cow with a calf charged out of some vines at Monte. He spurred the Brown who barely got out of way in time. He circled her as she stood defiantly and watched him. He gathered his lariat and got close enough and threw it. She dodged her head slinging her massive horns in a rough circle. But not quick enough. As the rope grew tight around her horns she charged the Brown with a loud bellow. The Brown easily avoided her and Monte guided his horse around a tree. The cow put on her brakes and Monte jumped off his horse and did a couple of half-hitches as soon as she hit the ground. Then he reached into his saddle bag and pulled out another rope and caught her hind legs. He then stretched her out and tied the rope to another tree. He left cow and calf like that for a couple of hours. When he went back a lot of her energy was gone and he was able to drive her toward the herd.

At night they were dog tired but came to life again after Short Bread fed them.

They were often fed beef and potatoes. Sometimes gravy and biscuits. They would sit around their fires and tell tales about that days work. Sometimes they talked of past experiences. One of the cowboys had a guitar that Red carried in his wagon. They were serenaded by his deep sounding voice. Sometimes they joined in when they knew the songs. Most of them had their own stories they could entertain with.

One month later they tallied their herd. One thousand and fifty. While they had been branding Monty had ridden to surrounding ranches and bought cattle. He offered them seven dollars a head and they were to deliver them on an agreed date to Monty's ranch. An undertaking that big could not be kept quiet. Word began to spread about Monty's aspiring enterprise. It was talked about in the Suds, the General Store, on the streets of Ludwig, and on neighboring ranches. Such talk was bound to fall on some bad ears. Baldy Burns and his bunch of toughs heard about it. They had just ridden into the territory after being run out of a town five counties away.

Immediately Baldy began to make plans. He had some bad information that said Monty had never bossed a trail ride before. They had been working for weeks out there in those breaks rounding up cattle. They must be awful tired at night. He heard about their branding the cattle and leaving them at his ranch. "Boys, he said, this is going to be easy pickings. I hear they have well over one thousand cattle already branded. We can take those cattle and kill as many of those hands as we can and then drive those cows for about 100 or so miles north of here and sell them. You all with me in this?" "Haven't we always been," said Limey Saint? "All right, we'll give it two nights and then the twelve of us will pay them a visit, said Baldy. He was a rough looking man with an unkept beard. He had a hawk nose and wore a dark crowned hat. His gun hung low on his hip and he talked with a snarl. He was somewhat heavyset but agile for his size.

The night they were to arrive, the crew had settled in for the night. The night riders were circling the herd. The sky was clear and the moon was bright. Monty had given instructions that no one was to be a hero. If they spotted trouble they were to let the whole crew know about it. They would handle it together. Monty had posted guards to watch for rustlers, for he knew the word would spread and that there would be someone who would try to take their herd. About midnight one of the nightrider's came ridding in on the run. He had spotted several riders skylined a short way off. Monty woke the crew and told them what was happening. They quickly saddled and mounted and rode to where Monty thought the rustlers would come in. He had the men to dismount and tie their horses to trees and brush and then they went further ahead and spread out. He told them to lay low and don't shoot until he did. Then he told them to fire at the gun flashes, then to the right and left of the flashes. He guessed correctly. His men were positioned and ready. Soon they heard the rustlers walking their horses to keep down their noise. But they had already been heard and spotted. Monty let them get out of the trees into a clearing. He was laying on the ground with his rifle ready. The rustlers mounted their horses and started walking them toward the herd.

Suddenly Monty broke the silence by yelling, "This is Monty Lane of the H/B Ranch and his riders. Your covered, so stop right there." A rustler's gun flashed and the bullet went over Monty's head. Monty answered back with his rifle and then his riders answered with him. Five would be rustlers fell. The others started to turn around and flee. The drover's guns sounded again. Three more riders fell. Then it was over. Monty yelled for his men to hold their fire and stay put. After fifteen minutes he yelled again for them to go back to camp. "Aren't you going to check them out," asked Lefty Gates? "Not now," said Monty, we'll wait for daylight. It'll be safer then." "But what if there's some wounded out there that need attention." Monty looked at Lefty and said, "we didn't invite them. They invited themselves, and they shot first. And they weren't shooting to scare us." 'We only did what they intended to do to us. And we still have our lives and our cattle." He turned and walked away.

    Luckily the cattle were far enough away they didn't stampede. The night riders had done their job well in keeping them calm.

    At daybreak Monty and Short went to check out the results of the night. There were eight dead riders lying out there. Monty instructed Short y to strip them of their gun belts, to search their pockets for money and identification and put it all in the supply wagon. They found most of their horses grazing not faraway. They led them back to the camp and added them to the horse remuda herd. He then told his riders to check their weapons against those confiscated and if they wanted to exchange with any of them they were welcome to it. The same was true of the horses. Monty saddled the Brown and rode to town to see the Sheriff. He found the sheriff at the Suds wetting his whistle and told him what happened. The Sheriff sat his mug down and said, "You killed eight men?" "Well, I sure didn't want them to kill me or any of us. We warned them and they shot first and we answered them." Then he wanted to know about the bodies and Monty told him there were right where they fell. "Why didn't you bury them," he asked? "Why," asked Monty. "Because it's the decent thing to do," said the sheriff. "Well I don't reckon they would have buried any of us," said Monty and he turned and left. When Monty returned to camp they dumped the bodies into an arroyo and pushed dirt on top of them.

Chapter Five

The round-up was finally over and the cattle branded. The horse herd was gathered, although they were harder to come by than the cattle. They also cost a lot more money. However, some of the riders had extra horses that they brought with them. And then there were the extra horses from the rustlers. Word spread about the rustlers failed attempt and the eight that were killed. Monte Lane suddenly became a name known as a man to leave alone. He was a hard man.

The rest of the herd arrived and Monty payed each rancher seven dollars a head. Nathan had already brought the Circle B's five hundred cattle.

Monty was about ready to mount BlackJack when he saw a rider coming toward them, riding fast and hard. Monty said to Nathan, "I wonder who that is? We're all ready to go and everyone is here. Nathan said to Monty, "It's you're friend." "What friend," asked Nathan. "Your lady fried, that little woman who likes to put her arms around you. She probably wants to hug you by." Monty looked at Nathan and said, "you are kidding me, aren't you? "I don't think so," said Nathan, as he grinned.

As Miss Vicky arrived, she dismounted and ran over to Monty. She looked up at him and asked, "Monty dear, were you going to leave me and not say good-by?" "I'll miss you Monty. I'll think about you every day you're gone."

With that, she stepped closer and reached up with her lips grabbed his shirt and pulled him down and kissed him.

With that some of the cowboys who didn't know what was going on began to whistle, and yell out things like, "Hey, sweetie, what about me?" "I'm next."

In Pursuit of a Dream | 39

someone yelled, "I get seconds," yelled another. Monty managed to break away from her, he took her arms from around his neck.

He looked at her and said, "Vicky, I don't know what possessed you to start this foolishness but you must end it now. Now. I don't love you. I love Beth and when we get back I'm going to marry her, understand? With that he turned and mounted his horse. As Monty started to ride away, he heard Vicky yell, "By Darling, I'll miss you and I'll be waiting for you when you return." With that she rode away.

It was time to begin. Monty rode back to the Circle B and told Beth and Nathan and the new crew "goodby." Nathan shook his hand firmly and gave him the map he promised him and wished him good luck. Beth tearfully hugged Monty "Good by." When I come back I will have a surprise for you," he said. "You mean your new ranch," she asked? Monty looked at Nathan. Nathan held up both hands and with a grin said "I didn't tell her, honest," he said. "How did you find out, asked Monte. She smiled at him and said, "Monty dear, there are some secrets that a girl just doesn't tell." He kind of snorted and shook his head as he took her in his arms and kissed her goodby. For a moment he held her tightly and then turned and mounted Blackjack and rode away. As she waved goodby to him she once again put her hands to her chest and tearfully said, "Please God, bring him back safely to me. Please! I love him so. Please keep the entire crew safe, Lord. Be their Protector in the midst of dangers. Amen." The next morning, daybreak found them all in the saddle, Tom Wells and Short Briggs started as the drag ridders, who whistled and swung their lariats to the cows behinds to keep the cattle moving at a good pace. There were two flank riders on each side, Curly Springs and Mack Shears on one side and Lefty Gates and Nathan Meyers on the other side. Sidney Meyers was riding point. Zeek Gage and Rife Stout looked after the remuda. Red started out driving the supply wagon and "Shortbread" the cook's wagon. Monty was their scout and trail boss.

He took his place well in front, took off his hat and waved it over his head and shouted, "All right, let's move'm on." The trail drive to Abilene had begun!

As they moved out not all of the cattle wanted to go. The cowboys were kept very busy trying to keep the herd together and moving. The drag riders were smacking their lariats hard against the cows backsides . When they lurched forward their horns encouraged those in front to move a little faster. The herd bawled their disapproval of this whole affair. There were many trail quitters who decided they wanted to return to the brakes. There were those on both sides that would decide they wanted none of this drive and bolted off to the side. Curley and Mack would dart after them, smacking them hard across their nose or backside with their lariats. They would bawl and head reluctantly back toward the herd. One big brown steer broke from the left side and Mack took out after it. The steer whirled and swung its big wide horns at his horse. Mack jerked his horse to the left and away just in time. He grabbed his lariat and called for Curley. He came and they both roped the steer, one the head the other the hind feet. Then they stretched it out and hogtied it. Just as Curly started for his horse he swung his lariat down hard on the beast's face and nose. Curly examined his horse and found no marks on him. He mounted and they rode back to the herd. As he continued on he looked back and saw the steer struggling and bawling. After about an hour he turned his horse around and rode back loosened the ropes on the steer and drove it on the run to the herd. It found it's place and remained there. At the front of the herd there were four steers who were striving for the lead. They would work it out but Monty had put his money on the brindle. Zeke and Gage were managing the horse herd with no problem. They had thirty mounts. Shortbread was driving his wagon behind, and off to the side as much as possible to keep out of the dust. Red Barton was driving the supply wagon beside Shortbread. Every little bit Red would whip the reins up and down and holler at his mules, "get up mules" to keep up with Shortbread. Shortbread would grin and tip his hat.

Monty had ridden about fifteen miles out when he found a good place to camp with water nearby and plenty of grass. He rode on for about twenty miles more, looking around for tracks and learning the lay of the land. Then he rode back to the herd and told Sidney, the point rider, to pass the word, about ten more miles and they would stop for the night. Monty kept his map handy that Nathan had drawn for him and referred to often for trail and water information.

There weren't any bad situations and the herd was moving along at a good trail speed. Finally, as it was turning evening they arrived at camp. "Let the horses drink first, then the cattle. Let them drink their fill and then drive them across," yelled Monty.

Shortbread drove his wagon down close to the water, eased his big red mules into the stream and then urged them across. Red followed, finding the stream was mostly rocky bottom with little mud. Once across, they unhitched their mules and cared for them. The cattle were so tired from the hard days drive that after they had drank their fill they lay down quickly and presented no problem throughout the night.

When it was dark Shortbread looked up at the stars to find the North Star. He then took the wagon tongue and pointed it north. The next morning when there were no stars in the sky he wouldn't have to guess which way was north. Then he started breaking out the cooking utensils. He built a fire from the kindling in the possum belly of his wagon. A couple of the riders drug some logs up to keep the fire going the rest of the night. The first item to make was coffee. Good, hot. strong black coffee. In the morning he could add egg shells to it. He then got out a huge black skillet and from a jar threw in some grease and started slicing beef into the skillet. Then he began washing potatoes. In another pot he poured water and beans. They were going to eat good tonight. That night Monty had them to tell about the day's events. Short told about the steer that tried to horn his horse. Monty commended him for his action, then said to watch out for this. "After they were on the trail a couple of days and you find one that is bad about it, when it tries it on you shoot it and leave it lay. "Shortbread, can you skin it and quarter it or do you want one of us to do it for you?" "I don't need no help, thank you," he answered. "Red and I can handle it. Can't we Red?" Red nodded in agreement. Thus far none of the crew had hinted at any negative feelings about having a blackman on the drive. They treated him with the same respect as they did one another. Their main concern was his ability to cook. And he did a good job of convincing them in that direction.

That night four riders were selected for the first night hawking. They would switch at three am. Everyone would be up at daybreak. Shortbread was to have breakfast ready.

The night was uneventful and everyone was so tired that they slept well, including the cattle. It would be one of the best nights on the trail.

Just before daybreak Monty rose first, except Shortbread, who had a fire going for coffee, and breakfast was cooking. Monty shook out his boots making sure there were no scorpions or snakes in them. Then he put on his hat and finished dressing. All the riders had their horses tethered nearby or secured to the rope line. Breakfast was quickly put behind them and they were mounting their horses. Several horses "crow hopped" to let their rider know their disapproval. The riders didn't mind. They said it showed the horse had spirit. The horses and cattle were up, watered and ready to begin the trail. Monty rode to the front and waved his hat forward. The horse remuda was behind him and then the cattle. Again the same four steers were striving for the lead. The brindle was still challenging for the lead. After a few days, he would emerge as the lead steer. And he would hold that position until the end of the drive. Sometimes a good lead steer would not be sold but brought back home to lead the next drive.

Two days later, in the afternoon storm clouds began to gather in the west. The wind picked up some. After a while Monty appeared and said there was a place to camp about five miles ahead. "Be sure to drive all the herd across the river and then let them drink. If it rains very much that river will rise and it could get swift. Too swift for us to cross."

Sidney rode back to the drag riders and told them to speed them up. They slapped the rears of the cattle who jammed those in front of them with their sharp horns, and so up the line. Sidney then rode back toward the point. As he passed the riders he pointed straight in front of him and they understood. He led them to the river. The horses were pushed across the small river and then cattle arrived and wanted to stop and drink but were pushed on across then allowed to return and line the bank to quench their thirst. Soon thunder was heard, not too far ahead and west. Monty told Shortbread to get supper over as quick as he could. That storm was moving in fast. Shortbread put his hands on his hips and said to him, "Mr. Monty, I know what to do." "Yes, sir," replied Monty, "I'm sure you do," He tipped his hat to Shortbread and turned the Brown around and rode off. He realized he had made a mistake. When a man knows his job he doesn't need to be told how to do it.

No sooner was supper over than the wind picked up considerably. Shortbread was trying to tie everything down he could. A tarp had been stretched from the cook's wagon to some poles. It flapped in the wind but held. Soon the sky was filled with wild jagged lightning. It was moving closer and closer. The thunder was rolling toward them. Monty yelled for all the riders to mount and start circling the herd. "But when they run, get out of their way. We just want to try to head them on up ahead. Don't get in front of them! Stay well off to the side."

The cowboys were swinging their lariats and trying to yell above the storm. Rain was pelting hard both man and beast. Then it began to come down in sheets and made it difficult to see. Cows were bawling nervously as they walked around. Then it happened. There was a wicked streak of lightning that struck the ground near the herd and a ball of fire rolled three feet. That did it! The cattle bawled and horses reared and neighed. Then horses and cattle all bolted ahead. Monty yelled, " stampede"!!! Luckily it was in the right direction for they were running hard. The riders tried not to ride to close to the herd but close enough to fire their guns and keep them heading in the right direction. Then there was another bolt of lightning that hit the ground on right side of the herd. They began to split in two directions, straight ahead and to the left. There was no stopping them so they let the cattle run themselves down. The storm continued into the night. Monty passed the word for all of them to return to camp. They would pick up their trail in the morning.

Finally, well after midnight the storm let up and the lightning stopped. At daybreak the crew crawled out from under the two wagons and bolted down their breakfast. After gulping down some hot coffee they headed for their saddles. Their horses had been secured before they turned in. They seemed to know it was going to be a long day. It was such a nasty morning there weren't many crow hops. Monty called them all in and gave instructions. Ride north until the tracks start to separate and then split up in twos and drive the cattle back to the main trail.

Monty and Lefty rode together and after a mile found twenty munching grass. They passed them up saying they could pick them up on the way back. They had ridden about five miles further and passed several small groups of cattle who continued to graze and pay them no attention. They continued on further west and then in the meadow ahead they saw a large herd. They estimated around two hundred head. But something was wrong with this picture. Lefty spoke to Monty, There" something wrong here boss. Those are our cattle and they aren't just walking this way, their being driven toward us. Somebody's pushing them and you and I are the only ones from our outfit over this far. Soon they counted eight or nine riders driving them. Monty and lefty rode to the side of one of the riders. "Thanks for heading part of our herd back toward us," said Monty as he tried to smile and be friendly.

The rider returned no friendly notions and only pointed to a man in a blue shirt riding a buckskin. Three other riders moved in beside and behind the man in blue. Monty knew this was the leader of the group and rode over to him and said the same to him. All four riders pulled up and formed sort of a semi circle and the man on the buckskin looked hard at Monte and said, "we ain't driving these cows for nobody but ourselves. These are our cattle."

"But they have our brand on them," said Monty. " Brands don't mean much across the border and that's where were taking them." By now two other riders had joined them, all of them facing Lefty and Monty. They had purposely positioned themselves with distance between them. Their hands were near their guns.

Monty looked at the man in the blue shirt and said, "Mister, these are our cattle. They stampeded last night during that storm and we aim to take them back."

"Well you can try," said the man on the buckskin as he turned his head and winked at one of his riders. That was his mistake. Just a glance away and when he looked back, Monty's pistol was in his hand.

Two of the outlaws started reaching for their guns and Monty's colt had fired twice before either of them cleared their holsters. Lefty had his gun out pointed toward the man on the buckskin. He started to point his gun toward Monty and Lefty let the hammer fall. His gun roared and the man rolled from the saddle. As Lefty's gun roared, so did Monty's twice more. So close together that it sounded as one shot. Two more rustlers fell from their horses and lay still.

One of the outlaws still siding the herd yelled, "Let's get out of here," and lit out for the nearby timber. Lefty started to raise his gun for a final shot but Monty said, "Let them go Lefty, they've already paid too big of a price as it is."

Monty got down and took their guns and gun belts. Then he told Lefty to round up their horses and hold them for the remuda. Later on they would search their saddle bags and take what was useful. It was a hard land with hard ways. The only law on the prairie was the law that could be enforced. Some day another way to settle disputes would come. But in this case Monty and Lefty was the law and they had just enforced it. The justice of the west had prevailed. These were their cattle and they would fight to the death to keep them. Although Monty was a young cattle man he had faced situations that took the savvy of a seasoned wrangler. Perhaps remembering what had happened to his pa had bent him a little hard. But many times Monty remembered a young boy all alone in the world looking down at his murdered father's body riddled with bullets.. . all in the back except the final bullet in his forehead. His father had stood for law and order in an unlawful land and uncertain time. No one came to his father's aid. So Monty had decided to delve out justice the way he saw it. For a time as a Texas Ranger, now on his own. Some times he knew he was too harsh and his judgement was severe. But sometimes he just reacted to the situation. Beth and Nathan had tried to help him and sometimes he could understand what they were saying. But Monty had grown up in another world and it was hard to put the two worlds together.

Monty and Lefty gathered the herd together and started them toward the trail. By the time they reached it in the afternoon they had rounded up several hundred plus. The other riders were just as fortunate in their gathering. By evening time they had accounted for all but five cows. In fact, there were a few mixed brands that they had picked up down in the area where the outlaws were. The horses had not wandered as far off as the cattle and were not difficult to drive back to the trail. They now had several more horses than they started with, picking them up from the would be outlaws. By this time the wagon had quite a collection of weapons, including pistols and rifles. Several of the outlaws had a cache of bullets in their saddle bags.

Monty decided to camp where they were and start the next morning. Everyone was glad. They were all worn out. Shortbread fixed a good meal with some fried apples as dessert and as always strong, hot, black coffee. It was hot enough to singe the hair off you're tongue.

Chapter Six

As they were eating a voice came from the darkness. "Hello in the camp." "Whose out there," called Monty. "I'm a man who is hungry and tired."

"Come on in and keep your hands where they can be seen." A rider walked his horse into the firelight, his hands clearly visible. "Step up and eat with us," said Monty. The man did. He told them he was known as Bart Henry and he was from Kansas way. He had no particular destination and wondered if they needed an extra hand. He was good on his horse and had worked with cattle before. He was a man just short of six feet. He wore a flat crowned brown hat and had a gun on each hip. He rode a good horse that was above average for most cow hands. Monty noted his hands were rough looking so he was used to hard work.

He moved with ease, but there was something about him that bothered Monte. He couldn't put his finger on it. But as he looked into the eyes of this new man there just seemed to be trouble staring back at him. Monte told him if he did hire on it would be for the duration of the drive, there would be absolutely no drinking and no gambling, until the drive was over. If they passed any towns on the way no one would be permitted to leave the herd unless they had his permission. The man looked at Monty for a moment or two then said, "O.K."

Monte extended his hand and said, "Bart Henry you've just been hired."

Each of the crew came and introduced themselves to the new drover. Sidney saw Monte standing to the side and in low tones said, "Boss, there's something wrong here. I've seen this man somewhere and all I remember is that it's not good news. I believe this man is trouble. When I place him I'll tell you." "O.K." said Monte. I have the same feeling, but let's not tell anyone. Let's just wait things out and see what happens."

Chapter Seven

The next morning the sun shone bright without a cloud in the sky. The riders roped their horses, saddled them, and then held on as they crow hopped around a bit before they settled down for the day. The new man was up and ready with the rest of them. Monty told the new man to ride drag for the day. Then he pointed their direction and waved his hat forward. The drive was on again.

Things went well for the next few days. The new man was working out. He was good at handling herd quitters. He didn't shy away when it came his time at night riding. One night Sidney and Bart had pulled the same night serenading the cows. As Sidney was circling the herd he came upon Bart. He was so intent on what he was doing he didn't hear Sidney come up behind him. Bart's head was tilted back and he had a bottle to his mouth. "Boss told us there was no drinking on this drive," said Sidney. Bart jerked his head around and said, "a man's got to have something to keep him awake." "Nevertheless, no drinking on this drive." Bart eased his horse close to Sidney's and said, "Well, you just better keep your mouth shut, if you know what's good for you," said Bart. "Is that a threat," asked Sidney? "Mister, I don't scare that easily," said Sidney. Bart drew his gun and stuck it up at Sidney's throat and said, "Neither does this, Mister."

"Go ahead and shoot," said Sidney. Bart, held his gun steady for a few seconds as if he was eager to pull the trigger and then put it back into his holster.

Sidney said, "You know, I've seen you somewhere, I just haven't figured it out yet, but it will come." There was a real mean look on Bart's face as he said to Sidney, "I'll tell you one more time mister, you better keep your mouth shut, or you'll be dead." With that Bart shoved his boot into the side of his mount and rode away. Talking to himself, Sidney repeated his words, "It'll come."

The next morning as the crew was preparing to push the herd on Monty happened to notice Bart looking at Sidney. It was not a casual look, Bart was watching Sidney with a hard look. Monte wondered what was behind it. He never said anything but made a mental note of it.

That evening after they had the cattle settled down they were having their evening meal Shortbread had cooked. All of a sudden there was a commotion at one side of the camp. Monte quickly went in that direction and saw Bart and Sidney rolling on the ground. Each man was trying to pound the other. Monte quickly stepped into the middle of them and pulled them apart and ordered them to stop it.

As Sidney started to turn away Bart swung a hard right that caught Sidney on the chin. He went backwards and fell. Monte turned on Bart and grabbed his arm and slung him around and hit him hard on his ear. Bart went down and stayed on his hands and knees for a minute and then got up. Monte grabbed him and said to him, "Mister I gave you an order to stop. And when I give an order you better listen. You understand that? "I'm sorry, boss, I didn't hear you."

Monty knew he was lying but didn't push it. You care to tell me what this was all about," asked Monty. "No, it's between us," said Bart. "Sidney?" asked Monte. "Like he said, "It's between us," said Sidney.

"If it happens again, it is no longer just between you. It becomes a matter for all of us. You understand? Both Sidney and Bart shrugged and started for their horses. "Now, we've got work to do so mount up and let's ride." Monty knew that Sidney was a good hand. He had worked hard and was loyal. Therefore, the trouble had to be with Bart Henry. Was it something from his past? Sidney said he had seen him before. Maybe he remembered. The rest of the day the drive went all right for a trail drive. There were no storms, nothing to spook the cattle, and no accidents.

That night as they all gathered for supper, Sidney was eating and all of a sudden it came to him. Bart Henry was an outlaw. He had seen posters of him. He had robbed a bank in Kansas and killed two people. Bart was now out night hawking. It bothered Sidney as to what to do. Should he confront Bart alone about this? Should he confide in Monty and let him handle it? Finally he reached a decision. This was a cattle drive. They all had a stake in it. He must decide what was best for everyone. He wasn't afraid to confront Bart Henry alone. But Monty had continually emphasized he was boss. He made the decisions when it affected the drive.

Sidney made his way over to Monty and sat down on the wagon tongue beside him. Monty looked at him and in a low voice said, "Sid, have you remembered about Bart yet?" Slowly Sidney nodded his head and said, "I have, that's what I'm here about." "He's a thief isn't he Sidney." Surprised Sidney asked, "How did you know?" "I just felt it in my bones. I guess it's a carry over from the Rangers."

Then Sidney told him about the poster he remembered seeing. "All right Sidney, you did the right thing. I'll handle it now."

Monty turned to Nathan and said, "Nathan would you go and relieve Bart Henry?"

Nathan got up and said, "Sure boss." In a short time Bart Henry rode in and stepped down from his saddle. He noted that Sidney was on the other side of the camp still eating his breakfast. "Boss, riders coming," said Red. They all looked up and about eight men were riding toward them. Bart Henry moved toward his horse. Monty turned toward him and said, "Stay where you are Bart." The outlaw noted Monty's hand near his colt. Knowing nothing of Monty aptness with a colt, Bart stopped because all of the crew was watching him. To make a draw now would be suicide.

The riders rode right into the trail drivers camp. The man in front wore a badge. He looked the crew over and said, "I'm Sheriff Dune from Cactus Point. A little town just south east of here. Last week we had us a bank robbery and we're still looking for him, You seen any strangers around? "What's this hombre look like?" asked Monty? "Don't know," said the sheriff. "He killed the only man who saw him. That was the teller. This killer took two thousand dollars from us."

Without any hesitation, Monty turned to Bart Henry and said, "Bart, you're the only man in this outfit I don't know. Is he talking about you? Bart stiffened and looked hard at Monty, "that don't make me no thief." "Well, let's have the sheriff take a look at that saddle bag you're carrying." Bart starred at Monty, "Nobody touches my saddlebag, my horse, or me. You got that." Monty's hand was near his colt handle. With a stern voice Monty warned Bart, "Bart, don't reach for that gun or I'll kill you." "You can try," said Bart as he grabbed for his gun. Monty had his gun out and hammer back before Bart cleared his holster. "Hold it Bart," said Monty. But Bart continued to bring up his gun and Monty let the hammer fall. There was a loud boom and Bart Henry backed up against his horse and stood there. He tried again to raise his colt but suddenly it was so heavy he couldn't hold it any longer. It pointed toward the ground, fired into the dirt, and Bart Henry fell forward, dead before he hit the ground.

No one moved for a moment. Then the sheriff asked, "Mind if I look in his saddle bags."

"Help yourself," said Monty. The sheriff stepped around the dead man and reached into the saddle bag. He found another gun, shells, and a burnt cinch ring.

But no money. Monty took a deep breath and held it. He walked around the other side of the saddle and reached into the saddle bag and pulled out a handful of money. He counted it. Not quite two thousand dollars. "Well, said the sheriff, I guess that does it. Monty expelled his breath and said, "Not quite," said Monty. "You and your men can burry him. We have a herd to start."

The sheriff looked at Monty and said, "He doesn't deserve burying, but since you helped us we'll do it."

Monty looked toward the crew and said, "All right men, we've got a herd to move so let's get at it. We're done here." They all moved toward their horses.

Chapter Eight

As the herd moved out it wasn't long before Monty rode several miles ahead and then pulled the black to a halt. These were unshod pony tracks. Maybe twenty five or thirty. He decided to follow them and see where they led. He kept his eye more on his surrounding than he did the tracks. There were stick marks like something was being dragged behind a horse.

He followed a little farther and found indians camped along a stream. Several were bent over a man in a travois. Monty rode into plain view with both hands up in the air, his palms out.

"Friend," he said, "friend." He had no idea if they understood at all. Five of the braves grabbed their bows and bent them with arrows aimed toward Monty. He continued to walk his horse toward them and stopped near the travoise. He slowly dismounted keeping his eye on the young warrior in the travoise that had bad rake marks on his body. Rake marks from the claws of a large animal. Part of his flesh was torn on his arms, shoulders, and his sides were bloody. Probably a bear thought Monty. He was lucky to be alive.

Monty pointed to the man and then himself and then back the way he had come.

"Medicine man," he said, thinking of Shortbread. "Come follow, ten miles, maybe," as he held up 10 fingers. They looked at one another, at the wounded brave, then at Monty. "No go," they said. "Him die." Then Monty pointed to himself then toward the direction of the drive and circled his hand back toward the brave. I … "I bring medicine man to you."

He wasn't sure they understood but they began to talk and make motions with their hands. It was clear they were not all in agreement. After talking it over among themselfs their leader pointed in the direction Monty had pointed and said, "go, bring medicine man, he must not let Running Bear die. He brave warrior." Monty swung into his saddle and turned the black around and laid down the tracks. He rode hard then slowed a bit then galloped the black again at top speed. Finally he saw the herd and he headed straight to Shortbread's wagon. He told him what was going on. Shortbread said, "You want me to patch up a redskin?" I never signed on to nursemaid any Redskins." Monty said, "Shortbread this young warrior is in a bad way. I don't know if you can save him or not but we got to try." Why do I got to try," asked Shortbread? "Because, I'm asking you as a favor to me." "Yeah, and what's to keep them from lifting our hair if I can't fix him up?" "Well, I guess nothing, but I believe you can do it." "We taking anybody with us", he asked? Well we might take Lefty and Red." "All right let me get my stuff. This has got to be the dangdest, most fool hardy thing I've ever done. If I get kilt I'm going to gut shoot you." Not knowing all the supplies he would need he decided to just take the wagon.

The four started back toward the way and just a few yards out of view they were met by six indians. They escorted them back to their camp. Much talking was going on among the escort and one kept looking at Shortbread's mules. Shortbread looked at Monty and made an ugly face at him. When they arrived. They all remained seated. Monty got off and pointed to Shortbread and said to the chief, "medicine man." The chief said nothing. Monty motioned for Shortbread to dismount and together they walked over to the wounded warrior. That he was in a bad way was evident. One indian stood between Shortbread and the wounded man. He didn't move. Shortbread went around him to the other side and looked down at the young warrior who was in great pain. He had lost a lot of blood. "I don't know." he said to Monty. "He's got a chance, but it's a slim one. I need some hot water." Monty gathered sticks and started a fire. The braves just watched. He got a pot from Shortbread's wagon and gathered some water from the stream.

Soon it was boiling and Shortbread began washing his wounds as best he could. Then he took salve they used on the horses's cuts and applied it to as many cuts as he could. He rolled the skin up in place and sprinkled it with medicine power and then wrapped it. Then he put a spoonful of laudanum into his mouth. The indian made an ugly face but swallowed it. Shortbread turned to Monty and said, "that's about all we can do for him now. He's going to have a fever soon. He needs some of our medicinal liquor. How do we keep it away from the rest of them?" "I don't know. We're on dangerous ground here," said Monty.

They walked away from the wounded brave and the rest of the Indians and sat down on some rocks to wait. After a bit they too sat down facing the white men.

During the night Shortbread was up several times seeing to the wounded brave. His fever was high. Shortbread gave him more whisky and laudanum. The next morning the brave opened his eyes. His fever had broken. He looked at his comrades and then at the whitemen with questions in his eyes. When one of the indians answered him, Monty knew he was their leader. Monty got "medicine man" out of it as he pointed toward Shortbread. Shortbread unrolled the bandages and put more medicine and new bandages on him. It was evident he was some better. His eyes were clearer and his face was some brighter. The pain was not as great. The "medicinal whisky" probably had something to do with that. Monty started to gather things up to leave. The one brave, who was the leader, took Monty's arm and said, "You stay, more day," he said as he held up one finger. Monty said, "We really need to get back to the herd," and he pointed back the way they had come. "No, you stay one day." Monty looked at Shortbread and he shrugged his shoulders. Monty said, "O.K. One day." He told Lefty and Red to walk slowly to their horses and return to camp. They started and got about five steps and three warriors stepped in front of them. Their leader said something sharply to them and they stepped aside. Monty gave them instructions to deliver to the trail drivers and to reassure them everything would be all right. As they left he and Shortbread gave the wounded man extra care that day for he wanted to leave the next day. Shortbread continued the "medicinal liquor" to keep the fever down. The indians shared with them their venison as they ate. Shortbread watched them eat and said to Monty, "Would you look at these indians eat! I'm sure glad I don't have to feed this group. They'd eat right through all of our supplies within a week." True to their word the next day the Indians allowed them to leave. Their leader pointed to himself and said, "Me Bear Claw, you friend," as he pointed to Shortbread and then to Monty. "Him Running Bear, very brave young warrior. Someday Great Spirit make our paths cross again." Monty and Shortbread nodded as they mounted and rode away. When they got a mile or so away Shortbread slapped his mules butts and Monty spurred Blackjack ahead. After a bit they slowed their pace. Shortbread turned to Monty and asked, "Monty what in the tarnation made you ride into those indian's camp like that. You could have got yourself shot full of arrows?"

Monty studied a moment and looking at Shortbread said, "I don't rightly know. I knew somebody was hurt pretty bad and I wanted to see if I could help. I'm glad I did Shortbread, and I really thank you for coming back with me." "Well, I ain't too sure just yet, we'll see after we get back into camp. This may just cost you extra." answered Shortbread.

The herd had continued to be pushed ahead though not at the same pace. Short had been the ramrod and had done well. Monty assumed his place as scout.

Everything went well for the next several days. On the tenth day after they had left the indians, they made camp and shortbread had fixed the evening meal with plenty to spare. It was a good thing!

As they were just getting started eating, Nathan nudged Monty and said, "Boss, we got company coming," as he pointed south west. Six indians were riding toward them at a slow trot. Monty recognized three of them and said, "Their from that tribe we helped the other day. He got up and walked to meet them and held up his hand. "Friend, come eat." he said as he gestured with his hand. They dismounted and Monty recognized one of them as the wounded man. His wounds were healing but still quite noticeable. Their leader was some kind of a chief and the others he did not know. One of them had been leading a horse laden with something covered with a buffalo hide. The wounded man walked over and pulled off the robe and there was fresh buffalo and venison. "You take," said the chief. Monty grinned as he reached out his hand to the chief who took Monty's forearm and they shook several times. "You speak good English," said Monty to the chief. "White man teach." "Well then how about something to eat." The chief spoke to those with him and they nodded their approval. They sat down apart from the crew and Shortbread served them."

"You got whisky? Asked the chief? "No," said Monty," No whisky." They frowned at Monty and said, "want whisky." Again Monty said to the chief, "No Whisky." The chief frowned and again said, "We want whisky." Monty was just as forceful as he answered back, "No! No Whisky," and he turned and walked away from them. Shortbread gave them plates of food and coffee and they began to eat, and eat, … and eat. Finally everything Shortbread had fixed was gone, plus all the coffee. Shortbread grumbled and took their plates and put them in the dishwater, He did start another pot of coffee, as he continued to mumble to himself, " If they stay very long they'll eat everything we got."

The chief spoke to Monty. "Much cattle, where go?" Monty pointed north and said, two moons." The chief pointed to wounded indian and said, "Running Bear want go with you. He be big help to you. Guide. No like cow. He pay back medicine man." Monty glanced around at his crew and saw several negative glances. Shortbread was frowning and slightly shaking his head. Monty said to the chief, "We will be honored to have Running Bear go with us." Monty knew this was risky and that the majority of his crew did not agree with him. But it was done.

The indians mounted their ponies and rode away leading the extra horse. Running Bear was very uncomfortable and walked over and sat down on the wagon tongue. "All right," said Monty, "It's time to get the night riders moving. As one of the riders started toward his horse he said to Monty, "I sure hope you know what your doing boss." Monty answered back, "It's my worry, and only mine." "Well, I ain't so sure about that," he answered. The night riders rode out. The next morning as the riders rolled out of their beds Running Bear was not found. "Sidney said, "He must have cut out during the night and gone back."

"Good," said Shortbread. "He didn't have any bottom when it came to eating. He et more than three men." They started the herd who by now were trail wise and not near as hard to trail. "We're going to push them for fifteen miles today. They won't like it and it looks like it might be a dry camp tonight," said Monty.

Monty had established his leadership among the men from the beginning. He was the owner and the trail boss. There were times when they disagreed with his judgement but they followed his orders. And he was most often right. That caused them to respect him even more. There were times that he would ask them as a group their opinion on matters. They worked together well. At the beginning they all had agreed to forty-five dollars a month plus fifty dollar bonuses when the cattle were delivered and sold. Monty had further promised them a job on his new ranch at forty-five dollars a month and found, when they returned. This was a security that appealed to all of them. That evening Running Bear rode in, straight to Monty. Without dismounting he said, "many riders ten mile out. They follow, watch herd. No good." "Well, your right about that," said Lefty. They sound like herd cutters."

Running Bear dismounted picked up a piece of cooked buffalo, mounted again and said, "Me watch," and he was gone.

Red spoke up and said, "Boss, I sure thought you made a wrong decision back there but maybe it wasn't so wrong after all. That "injun" is a big help to us." Several of the men shook their heads in approval.

Two days later Running Bear caught up with the herd and rode to Monty. He made fists and opened them twice and said, "riders close, maybe five miles. They send riders to watch cows. They hold big powwow."

"Well, that means they will probably strike tonight or tomorrow.

Running Bear said, "I watch," then he was gone. Monty notified each rider of the bad news and told them to stay ready. The rustlers would stampede the herd and then try to shoot them out of the saddle. Monty told each man to be careful and not get caught up in the herd. Ride well to the side of it and turn your attention to the rustlers. Shoot to kill. Show no mercy, understand, no mercy. If they come at night shoot at the flashes. Once at the flash, then to the right, and then to the left. He instructed each man to have plenty of shells for his weapons. Some of them were carrying an extra gun in their waistband.

When they stopped for the night everyone was on edge. Especially the night riders. However, the night went without incident. At daybreak Running Bear rode into camp and said, "They come, " pointing the direction they would come. "Probably figure they have us outnumbered and that we will run. All right, men this is it. Get ready," yelled Monty as he swung his leg over his saddle. They mounted their horses and drew their rifles and rode out. All of a sudden Monty whistled and waved his hat for all the riders to come in. They rode to him and he said, "Red and Lefty, you stay with the herd. The rest of us are going to take the fight to them. They looked to the south-west and could make out a cloud of dust. "Looks like we're too late for that. All right, gentlemen find you a place to stand. Get a tree, a wallow, on your horse, or on the ground but get set. They will probably stop to look us over then try to run over us. Don't shoot until I do." The men scattered, three of them got into the supply wagon and laid down. Two more got under the wagon. One was behind a tree. Monty was kneeling on the ground with his rifle ready. Soon the riders appeared and stopped a hundred yards off. When they saw their surprise attack lost and the element of surprise gone, they kicked their horses charging straight at Monty and his crew. Both sides knew this was not going to be as easy as expected. The over anxious rustlers started firing way too soon to be effective. A man riding a horse going up and down cannot shoot as accurately as a man standing still with a steady aim. Monty waited until they were close. He put his aim right on the front rider as his shot zinged past Monty. Monty squeezed the trigger on his long gun and the man fell, never to get up again. All the M/B riders guns opened up and three more saddles were emptied and two horses fell. Their riders scrambled to find a safe place. The rustlers turned and rode a short distance away then a second time they charged the M/B riders. The trail drivers again opened up with their weapons and three more saddles were emptied. By now they were among the M/B riders who had placed themselves in places where they were well protected. Their guns were blazing with deadly accuracy and more saddles were emptied. The rustlers decided this was more than they bargained for and turned their horses around to ride away. Remembering what Monty had said about no mercy, the M/B riders fired again as the rustlers attempted to ride away. Another rustler left his saddle and lay still. The rest of the herd stealers were leaning low in their saddles and kicking the sides of their mounts hurrying away as fast as they could go.

Monty rode out to see about the men shot, they were all dead or dying. One of them cursed him and tried to lift his gun but was unable. As Monty looked at another, the rustler looked up at Monty and said, "You got me good, Mister." Looking down at him, Monte said, "We didn't invite you to breakfast." "We figured you were a bunch of green horns and that you would scare easy." Then he took his last breath. Monty gathered their weapons and told one of the crew to round up any of their horses still around and put them with the remuda." Anybody get hurt. "Nathan got a scrape of a bullet on his leg, and Short got one on his arm, but that's about it," said Lefty. Good, I'm glad no one was hurt bad," said Monty. "All right, let's go back to camp," said Monty. When they arrived. Shortbread had the coffee going and breakfast ready. The men all ate and started for their horses to once again round up the scattered herd that had scattered when the shooting began. "Dagnabit, seems like we spend most of our time rounding up this herd, instead of pushing it," said one of the riders. "Well, that's the joy of a trail drive," answered another. "There aren't any guarantees, it's always a gamble. Just be glad we haven't been hit by any indians, or that we haven't run out of water."

Chapter Nine

The day passed without incident, except for Monty and Lefty. It appeared the cattle hadn't run too far nor scattered as much as other times so they took time for breakfast before going after the cattle. Shortbread laid out biscuits with honey, thinly sliced beef, and some brown gravy on top. The men quickly ate and then headed for their horses, and started for the herd. "Well, your guess is as good as mine as how bad the scatter is so lets pair up and start looking. Hopefully they haven't gone too far."

The gather wasn't as bad as other times except for Monty and Lefty. They rode forward and west about three miles and then noticed a number of tracks that led west. They followed until they came to a wide stream and good grass. There ahead of them was a large herd. Let's pass them by and pick them up on the way back," suggested Lefty. "I hope this isn't a repeat of another time," said Monty. On up ahead there was a big object over near the woods. It wasn't a cow. As they approached closer it disappeared into the woods. They both headed toward it. At the edge of the woods they found a dead cow, freshly torn apart. Something had already eaten part of her. Wolves?" asked Lefty. "No, said Monty as he pulled his carbine from its scabbard and cocked it. See those tracks. Those are bear tracks, and big ones. My guess is he's in there watching us right now." Slowly they started to back their horses away when suddenly there was a loud growl and a big rush of something big coming through the woods right at them. Saplings parted, mesquite snapped and bushes were pushed aside as an invisible animal of tremendous power rushed toward them. There was another a big growl as a massive brown bear bolted out of the underbrush charging right at them snapping his jaws as he charged. Lefty's horse spooked and turned sideways to run but the bear made a swipe at him with his big paw and struck the animal on the flank. The horse screamed and was knocked sideways to its knees. Lefty was trying to kick himself free of the stirrups. His horse lost its balance and fell on it's side. Lefty went rolling away from his horse and the bear. Perhaps because the horse was a bigger meal the bear again and again clawed the horse biting its weathers. Monty snapped off a shot into the bear. His bullet went into the back of its shoulder. The bear howled and turned toward Monty who was still mounted on the brown. His horse was trying to fight Monty's hold on him and get away. Monty jumped off the Brown and landed facing the bear. The bear charged Monty not thirty feet away. The hair was standing up on its neck and its mouth was open. It's large teeth snapping ready to rip his intruder to pieces. He looked like a huge monster of death. Monty pumped three shots into the bear as quickly as he could work the lever of his rifle and pull the trigger. One shot ripped into the bear's lung, another into his heart, and the last was right between the eyes. Then Monty flung himself to the right and rolled three times before he attempted to come up with his rifle ready to shoot again. Lefty had also opened up with his rifle and the bear staggered and then fell, his huge claws reaching as he fell. He landed with his front paws not more than three feet from Monty. Standing there with his rifle still pointed at the bear Monty found himself unable to move. Neither man could move for five long minutes. Both men felt somewhat weak in the knees. Monty sank to his knees, his rifle still cocked and ready. He was unable to speak. Lefty walked over and kicked the bear ready to fire if it moved. Still neither man was able to say a word. Both were breathing hard. Finally, Lefty said, "Man, I sure thought I was a goner that time. I thought St. Peter was beckoning me to the pearly gates. You sure saved my bacon boss." I thought I was a goner too," said Monty. " He had so much momentum going for him I thought sure he was going to topple right on top of me."

 Finally both men regained enough strength to walk around the bear. Not being too sure, Lefty took his toe and pushed it again on it's rump, but it was dead. Monty whistled for the Brown who came trotting back to him but stopped short when he saw the bear and smelled its blood. He shook his head up and down and then reared about half way snorting at the strong smell of the bear. Monty walked toward him and talked softly to him. He reached the Brown with no problem and led him a little ways away and told him to "stay."

Lefty looked at his horse and asked, "You reckon that horse of yours will ride double? Mine's done for. He's hurt too bad to carry me." "I doubt mine will carry double," said Monty. "He's a one man horse." "Tell you what, Lefty, walk back toward that stream and I'll ride down it further and see if there are any horses that way." Lefty checked his rifle and reloaded it full and checked his short gun also. Then he pointed his rifle at his horse and pulled the trigger and it suffered no more. Then he began to strip the saddle and bridle from it. Monty mounted the brown and started farther down stream. After about thirty minutes he saw some horses and lots of cows munching on the green grass. He took his lariat and slowly made his way to the far side of the horses. He recognized one horse as being somewhat gentle and made his way toward it. He got to ten feet of it and dismounted and walked toward it talking slowly and gently with a hand full of grass in his hand. The roan stretched out it's neck and took the grass while Monty rubbed his neck and slipped his rope around it. He then made a hitch on its nose and led it back toward the Brown. He mounted and started the cattle and horses back toward where he left Lefty. Lefty was waiting for him, with his saddle stripped from his horse. He quickly threw his saddle on the horse and they started the horses and cows back toward the main trail and then they turned their horses around and started looking for more cows. After about an hour they found several small herds munching together not paying any attention to them. Finally, they decided they had ridden far enough and turned and started back driving their cattle and horses toward the main trail joining those they had seen earlier.

Chapter Ten

That evening Monty had the riders to take a tally of the horses and cattle. All but two of the horses were accounted for and they were only about 15 short in the cattle and that could be a miscount. As they sat around the fire that night Lefty began telling of their incident with the bear. When he told how close it was to Monty before it was stopped, they all gasped. Running Bear was sitting on the wagon tongue away from the group but he was listening. He looked at Monty and recognized him as a "Great warrior, "he kill bear." Monty looked over at their cook, "Hey Shortbread?" When the cook answered him, Monty yelled, "Shorty wants to know if you'll cook some of that bear meat tomorrow night. Shorty yelled right back, "You tell that scoundrel if he wants any of that bear meat to skin it and cook it himself. I'll have nothing to do with it." Everyone laughed, except Shortbread.

For the next week the trail drive went without incident. But that kind of luck can't hold out forever. One night, the night hawkers were out and the herd was uneasy. They refused to lie down and rest. They bawled and milled around. There was a slight breeze. Then not very far away there was the scream of a cougar. The slight breeze was just enough for cougar scent to be blown among some of the cattle. After a couple of minutes the second scream was close enough that it caused the cattle to all break into a bawling run. "Stampede," yelled the night riders. They rode as hard as they could firing their guns into the air to try to keep the herd from separating. The M/B riders around the camp saddled their horses as quickly as they could and rode after the herd. There was nothing they could do but let them run themselves down. They probably won't run very far anyway. Finally Monty fired his gun into the air several times and the crew made their way back to him. "Everyone all right," he asked. No one was hurt. Just mad as an upset hornet at those skidish cows. "We might as well get some rest and gather them up in the morning," said Monty. Two days later Monty estimated they had only lost around a dozen cattle. They drove the gathered cattle on and made another fifteen miles that day and came to a river that had some steep banks. Monty had ridden ahead and waved his hat to drive them west where the banks were not as steep. After they crossed and had their fill of water, they began to graze. The men were all tuckered out and the cattle too. The night went without incident and the next day Monty checked his map again that Nathan had given him. He had ridden about twenty miles ahead and then returned to tell them there was no water and they would have to make a dry camp that night. When they came to a place where the grass was more plentiful Monty halted the herd. Shortbread pulled off to the side, unhitched his mules and took the wagon tongue and pointed it north. The cattle were restless. They had traveled all day with no water, just eating the dust they had created. Just before noon they were traveling down the side of a hill and Shortbread failed to see a deep rut with a rock in the bottom of it. The rear wheel dropped and hit the rock hard. The wagon came to an abrupt halt. Shortbread grabbed his pistol and pointed it towards the clouds above and fired it up into the air. The flank riders turned in their saddles and saw Shortbread waving his hat. One of them galloped his horse back and found out the problem. He rode off and got a couple hands and they began the task of fixing the wheel. Fortunately there was another wagon wheel in the other wagon that would fit that one. Quickly they got the wheel out and rolled it down by the broken wheel. Then they began the task of lifting the wagon high enough to fit the new wheel in place. In order to do that they would have to lighten the load in the wagon. Shortbread wasn't very happy about that, but it couldn't be helped. Sometimes not being able to do something that appears to be simple and it turns out to be hard is far more frustrating than trying something hard in itself. One of the hands got under the wagon and raised his back up. He grunted and then strained some more.

Another hand shoved an eight inch log under the wagon until it was jacked up high enough to finish the job. Shortbread rolled the other wheel in place and Short started putting it all back together and tightening the wagon nut until it was tight.

The whole incident took about an hour and a half. Shortbread was angry at himself for the delay. Monty, who was near, heard Shortbread berating himself for the delay. He told Shortbread to not be so hard on himself. "Every man on the trail drive had his own moments when things didn't go right. Blaming ourselves wouldn't right one wrong or a dozen. He had to take it in stride and put it behind him.

Shortbread swung his long whip above his mules heads as he sat down in the wagon seat. It popped loud over the heads of his mules and he hollered "Git, You hear me, mules, I said, "Git," and he popped his angry whip just above the mules rumps. They leaned into the harness and brayed their displeasure at the sound of the whip. Once again Shortbread popped his whip over the heads of his mules and yelled, "Git along mules. Git I say. Git."

The delay made Shortbread late in preparing for supper that night but it couldn't be helped. The drovers all understood. When Monty walked up to get his plate Shortbread said to him, "Mr. Monty, I sure am glad we had that extra wheel." He grinned and said, "So am I Shortbread, so am I." It looked like a peaceful evening. However, for some reason the cattle bawled and refused to lay down. The night riders kept riding around them, singing to them, talking to them, trying to sooth them. It was a long night. Each man slept with his clothes on and his horse nearby saddled, in case they ran. But they didn't. At daybreak Shortbread had fixed a good breakfast and lots of coffee. After everyone had eaten Monty said, "Let's mount up, we're burning holes in our saddles. They mounted up and started moving them out. The big Brindle steer took his place in leading the herd.

Monty rode on ahead in search of water. Finally, about fifteen miles away he found a small stream. He looked it over and decided he had no choice but to make camp here. He rode down stream away's and stopped "the brown," short. He got down and studied the tracks. Unshod ponies. Many tracks. He looked at where they entered the stream and where they went out on the other side. Then he followed a short distance. They were not walking or trotting their horses, they had them in a gallop. Where were they going in such a hurry? Were they returning from a hunting trip, were they a raiding party, had they attacked another tribe or any settlers nearby? He decided to trail a little ways. About three miles further on the tracks split into two groups. One rode off to the right which might mean they were getting ready to circle something or someone. That was enough for Monty. He turned his horse toward east and started the Brown at a hard gallop.

Suddenly an indian pony came riding toward him. Monty pulled his pistol and took aim. Just as he was ready to squeeze the trigger he saw it was Running Bear. Running Bear had followed the tracks that led east. He told Monty that they would attack the wagon, probably at dawn. "Why not tonight," asked Monty. "Have big powwow tonight for big medicine, then attack."

They both started for the herd at a hard gallop. When they finally reached the herd Monty motioned with his hat to move the cows faster. They bolted and and bawled kept on bawling to show their dislike. But the riders kept them moving and bunched. Finally they reached the stream and spread a long ways up and down the stream, satisfying their thirst. Monty passed the word to get them on the other side a good ways away from the stream, the grass was good there. When they got the cattle and horses watered and settled down, Shortbread had gathered some sticks from the "possum belly" and had a fire going. Soon he had supper cooking. When it was done Shortbread shouted to the crew, "All right, you lazy loafers, it's ready, get up and start eating before I throw it out." They all jumped up and started grabbing plates and silverware. In no time they were hungrily chawing down. As the men ate Monty shared with them the news about the tracks he had seen and how they had separated. " My guess is that there were about forty indians all together."

"Is that all," asked Nathan? He jabbed a rider near by in the ribs and said, "Why we could handle them all by ourselves." "Yeah," said Short, "We'll remember that."

Before dawn the M/B riders were up and ready. Some were under the supply wagon, some were behind trees, some were laying on the ground, a couple were behind Shortbread's wagon. Shortbread was under the wagon with both a long gun and a short gun. Running Bear was near Monty. The early morning air was suddenly filled with cries and yells of indians as they raced toward the camp. Most of them had only bow and arrows so the H/B riders had their rifles ready because they would carry farther than their short guns.

Those on the ground fired first and three indians fell from their ponies. As the indians continued to charge those in and under the wagons fired. Six more indians fell from their horses and they still were not close enough to shoot an arrow. They turned around and rode out of rifle range and stopped. It was clear there was an apparent disagreement between warriors. Then with their element of surprise gone and the loss of nine of their braves they decided the white man had greater medicine than theirs and they rode back in the direction they had come.

Lefty asked, "reckon they'll be back?" "Maybe, maybe their going for reinforcements, keep your eyes open and your guns ready," said Monty.

"All right, let's gather the herd and get started said Monty. Shortbread came to Monty and asked, "Is there a town anywhere near here? I'm running out of some things like flour, beans, bacon, and some other things." Monty studied Nathan's map and said, "It looks like another ten miles and then off to the west about five or ten miles. ShortBread, You want to start off toward it now or wait until tomorrow?" "Why don't we go now. We never know what tomorrow's going to bring. I'll start now, that way you can catch up with me by evening?" "All right, said Monty.

He rode to the riders and told them where he and Shortbread were going and asked if they needed anything. Some of them said they sure would like some tobacco, but that was about it. All alcohol was forbidden while they were on the drive.

Monty told them to keep going and he would catch up with them later. He switched to the black gelding and rode off with Shortbread.

Shortbread rolled his wagon into town and stopped at the local general supply store. It wasn't much of a town, just a few buildings that cried out for paint. It had a run down looking saloon, a general store that carried groceries, some rifles, ammunition, some farm supplies. Off on down the road it looked like they had an entertainment house. They went inside the general store and the manager looked at Shortbread then at Monty. Monty caught his eye and said, "We have a list of supplies, would you fill them while we go and have us a drink." "You can go, but he doesn't come inside," said the proprietor pointing at Shortbread. Monty stiffened up with hands on his hips but Shortbread took his arm and said, "It's all right Mr. Monty, I'm used to it. Let him fill the wagon himself," said Shortbread.

The owner said, "I'll do that to keep you both from coming back in here." Monty's eyes narrowed and anger showed in his tone as he said, "Mister, you got off lucky this time." They turned and walked out. Monty entered the saloon first pushing the bat wing doors back, and Shortbread followed. The

In Pursuit of a Dream | 69

bartender eyed them and then said to Shortbread, "you go back outside and come in the back door. There's a table in the back there and I'll serve you there." Monty spoke up and said, "he's with me. He came in with me and he stays with me. His money is the same color as mine." Three men at the bar turned and looked at them and one took a few steps to one side. Looking at Monty, he said to Monty, "You heard what the bartender said, we don't serve his kind in here. Now you do as he says or we'll make you wish you had." "If your thinking of pulling iron on me, I wouldn't," said Monty. " You wouldn't clear your holster." One of the gents sitting at a table laughed and said "Mister, you don't know these two hombre. Their the fastest guns around here. I'd listen to them before you get hurt." Shorbread tugged at Monty's sleeve and said, "Its O.K. Mr. Monty. Like I said, "I'm used to it and I don't want to cause no trouble." "We're staying," said Monty. "We've been on the trail quite a spell and we're going to have us a drink." It wasn't the drink that Monty protested. He was standing for the right of his black friend to drink with him. They weren't bothering anyone. Monty, turning his eyes toward the two gunmen said, "When your ready gentlemen." The one at the bar started to draw first then quickly stopped and slowly lifted his hands upward. The other two men did the same. Monty had both of his guns drawn and pointed at them. "Put your guns on the bar nice and easy." He watched them closely as they laid them on the bar. "Now step away from them. O.K. Mr. Bartender, if you have a "greener" laying under neath on that shelf, go ahead and grab for it, if you feel lucky. If not, we'll have that drink." The bartender slowly turned around and took a bottle from the shelf and poured them a drink. After they had quenched their thirst Monty paid for their drinks then touched his hat to them and said, "Gentlemen, it was a pleasure. By the way, what harm did it do for our having a drink in here? I remember hearing a preacher once saying that, "Jesus wasn't a white man." Then Monty and and Shortbread backed out of the saloon and headed toward the general store. They turned a couple of times and looked back but no one was following.

 Still, they kept watching their back as they walked down the boardwalk but saw no one trying to dry-gulch them. Their wagon was loaded when they got there and Monty went in and paid the man as Shortbread readied the mules to go. As they drove out of town several men were standing in the saloon door watching them drive out of town. "We just might have to watch out for them tonight," said Monty. They caught up with the herd and that evening as they ate supper. Monty told them about the incident in town and to stay prepared for a showdown. "Let them come," said Nathan, "and we'll show them what tangling with this outfit is like."

"That's right," said another. "Shortbread is one of us."

The night riders mounted and relieved those circling the cattle, watching for anything that might seem suspicious. However, there was no incident during the night. The next morning they were in the saddle at daybreak starting another day. Running Bear was gone as usual. Monty rode on ahead and about twenty miles north he halted the Brown and stared at the horse tracks. All unshod. He turned and followed them a ways and then they parted. Some going back southwest and the others northeast. Those that turned south west could be circling back to hit their outfit for the horses. They had quite a large horse herd now.

The tracks that went northeast could be circling to set up an ambush. Just as he started to turn his horse around he heard a horse coming toward him from behind. He grabbed his six shooter and swung around but held his fire. It was Running Bear. He looked at Monty's pistol and grinned. "No shoot, whiteman, me good indian," he said with a grin.

He shared Monty's worry about the circling indians. "Are they from the same war party that attacked us before," asked Monty? Running nodded his head indicating "yes." Then they both spurred their mounts back toward the herd. When they reached camp he held up his hat for them to stop the herd. Most of the riders rode into camp while a few remained with the herd. As they all gathered around the camp fire he relayed to them what he and Running Bear suspected. "Be on your watch," said Monty. The men then rode back to the herd and told the others what was going on. Each man checked his side arm, spinning the cylinders and adding an extra shell to the safety chamber. Then they shucked their rifles and made sure the magazines were full. Many of them loaded a second gun and stuck it in their gun belts.

They then pressed on with the drive watching their back trail and on both sides. They made another fifteen miles that day and camped on the far side of the stream. After supper Monty posted double guards on the horse herd. Everyone else slept with their clothes on and their horses saddled. Before daybreak, Running Bear tapped Monty's arm. As Monty opened his eyes Running Bear said, "They come, be here soon. " How many," he asked as he was struggling with his boots. Running Bear held up both fists and then opened them two times. He pointed to the north and made the same motion. "Forty of them. Their going to hit us from both directions?" Monty quickly rallied the crew into readiness, including those keeping watch on the remuda. He said he thought that this would be their major attack.

The indians came from both directions. However, they had again lost their element of surprise and before they were in range with their bows and a few old rifles the M/B riders cut loose with their carbines. Several ponies were suddenly riderless, as the indians fell to the ground clutching their chests, shoulders, and their middles. But on they came with determination to get the horses. Again the rifles of the M/B crew sounded. Again and again with rapid fire and deadly aim. Indians fell with each volly of fire, but on they came yelling and leaning on the far side of their horses making themselves difficult targets. They were magnificent horsemen. As one looked at them they wondered what kept them from falling off to the ground. They were close enough now to loose their arrows. Two struck the side of the cook's wagon. Another three hit the supply wagon. One with fire struck the cook's wagon. Nathan quickly reached up and jerked it down. But before he could get back under the wagon an arrow caught his left arm. He dropped and rolled under the wagon and kept firing, even though it felt like flames of fire searing his arm. The riders that were guarding the horse herd realized they were no match for these marauding indians and had to seek better shelter and let the horses go. A large force of indians were firing their old rifles and their arrows with amazing accuracy. Though not striking any of the horse herd guards they struck very close.

The M/B rifles were firing so fast that their barrels were smoking hot. Indians in both parties fell from their horses in large numbers. But they had an objective to capture the horse herd and nothing could deter them from this task. Nothing but death itself. They drove the horse remuda north. Many of the cattle was spooked as well but they weren't interested in them. The M/B crew kept firing at the indians until they were out of range. Monty now on his Brown called the crew together. Everybody all right?" he asked. Nathan took an arrow in his arm and Short got one in his leg. I think that's about it, said one of the riders. Shortbread put some water on to heat. "Bring them over here," he said. He took his knife and cut a circle around each arrow and broke them. Then he gave both men some "medicinal whisky" they had brought back from town. When they were well soaked with it, he gave them a stick to bite down on and took the butt of his gun and drove the arrows on through. The pain was so intense that both men passed out. Shortbread then doused their wounds with more whisky and bandaged them. "Put them in Red's supply wagon, their going to need some rest," said Monty. Then he added, give them some more laudanum when they wake up. They spent the rest of the day rounding up the cattle. That evening Monty said to his crew, "Men we've got to get those horses back. I think tonight might be the best time to do it. They won't be as apptd to be looking for us tonight. They'll have guards posted so we'll just have to be extra careful. This can be a stamp and fool hardy gamble so if any of you choose not to go, it's all right." Practically all of them spoke at once saying, "I'm in."

That night Running Bear led the M/B riders near where the indians were camped. They surveyed the situation and decided to circle them to where all the horses were kept. Slowly the led their horses up to the Indian horse remuda. As they moved their horses closer and closer to the remuda, "Now, said Monty, and they all gave out a yell and jumped on their horses. They yelled and waved their arms stampeding all the horses toward the middle of the camp. Braves ran out of their tepees and then ran and jump around avoiding the fleeing horses. However, some of the braves managed to jump on the back of fleeing horses and kept them from running off. After the drovers had driven all the fleeing horses several miles beyond the middle of the Indian camp they stopped and dismounted and made a rough count of their horses. Afterward, Monty said, "Mount up and spread out. When I fire, make all the noise you can and scare these Indian ponies as far from that Indian camp as you can. If we do enough damage they will think our medicine is too strong for them." Maybe they will leave us alone for a bit."

Monty touched the Brown in the flanks and he bolted forward. Then he raised his colt upward and fired and yelled like a madman at the horses. The rest of the riders did the same and spread out as they rode. The horses bolted in the direction they wanted them to go which was right through the middle of the indians' camp. The indians had a difficult time defending themselves and avoiding being trampled by the frightened horses. Gunshots were fired as the riders sped through the camp. Curley fired point blank at one indian who had his bow drawn but never got to release it. Instead his arms went wide apart as his chest immediately became red. Mack was leaning low in his saddle and saw an indian point his pistol toward a rider and shot him in the side. The indian gripped his side and fell to the ground and lay still. Then it was all over. They were through the camp and they kept on driving the horses north toward their camp. They not only had their herd back but they also picked up a number of the indian ponies. They pushed the horses until they could see the outline of their camp. They doubled their watch for the night, and ground hitched their mounts and turned in. They were beat. Sleep came quickly that night. But nothing happened.

The next morning came early, as it always did. Running Bear came riding in as they were getting ready for breakfast. He took a plate from Shortbread and spoke to Monty. "Indians powwow to decide what to do. Monty said, "Do, what can they do, we scattered their horses and many of their braves, as well." "No," said Running Bear. We only hit small herd. Main herd on other side of camp. Monty frowned, scratched his head and then said, "Well you know if we could hit them hard again they would probably leave us alone." Running Bear grunted in agreement. Monty yelled and made the motion to "mount up." He explained what they had to do and left a few men at camp. As they neared the indian camp they slowed their horses to a fast walk. Running Bear had gone on ahead of them. He met them about a mile from the Indian's camp and told them the powwow was still going on with some of the braves dancing to cause the spirits to deliver the white men into their hands. They were about a fourth of a mile out when they were spotted by the indian guards. They quickly mounted their ponies and the warriors charged toward the whites, yelling and screaming in their charge. But their bow and arrows, their spears and axes were no match for the white man's repeating rifles. They were quickly shot down and forced to retreat. They were not pursued but instead the cattlemen pursued their efforts to drive the main herd of horses away from camp.

Then the rest of the indians knew they were unprepared and had little chance without their mounts and scattered into the woods and hills. Monty did not pursue them. Instead he motioned for the riders to circle and return to camp. They found everything O.K. at camp and Nathan and Short were very sore, but their wounds would heal with time and care. They still would not able to ride for a while.

The next day as Monty was scouting fifteen miles ahead he saw a cloud of dust moving toward him. He took out his field glass and determined the cause to be that of the U.S. Cavalry. They were heading in their direction. He rode to meet them. There were about twenty of them riding two abreast. He reined up Blackjack and waited for them. The Captain and he exchanged greetings and then the Captain asked Monty where he was headed. He then told the Captain about his drive to the nearest railroad to deliver twenty five hundred head of cattle. "Don't you know your in indian territory," he asked. "Yes sir," said Monty, we've already tangled with them and I think they'll leave us alone. How far to the fort Captain?" "About twelve miles straight ahead. "Thanks," said Monty. The Captain warned him about rustlers as they got closer to cattle towns. They waited for such herds to arrive close and then attacked, killing everyone they could. Monty thanked him for the information and turned his horse around and headed back for the herd.

They made ten miles and found water and grass so they camped there for the night.

Chapter Eleven

The next morning Monty told Lefty to keep them headed west and he would join them later. He mounted Blackjack and headed for the fort. He was stopped at the gate by a young soldier who probably was too young to shave. His voice was still struggling to sound like a man. He was a slender built youth of about five foot and ten inches. His blue eyes and blond hair went well with his uniform. "Who are you and state your business," he said. Monty gave his name and said he needed to see the post commander. "And your business sir." I have some prime horses for the army," said Monty. Shading his eyes, the soldier said to Monty, "I don't see any horses, Sir." Monty grinned and said to the soldier, ""If you don't let me see your General you won't see any new mounts." "May I ask who wishes to see the commander, Sir?" "I do," said Monty impatiently, "Just tell him there is someone out here who wishes to sell the army some good horses."

As the young private turned away, Monty said to him, "Good horses mind you," The young private hollered down for them to open the gate and let the stranger pass. After some moments the gates were opened and Monty rode through into the fort. He spotted what he thought was the Commander's office and rode Blackjack to the hitching rail and dismounted. He was met by a soldier who escorted him to the major. The Major was sort of a heavy set man of about forty with greying hair. As Monty stepped inside the Commander's office, he did not bother to get up. Instead he looked at Monty with his dark eyes and asked in a rough voice "What can I do for you, young man?" Monty explained about the trail drive and then said, Sir, I've got a ranch back home and I have some really fine mounts for the army if your interested in good horse flesh." Actually Monty didn't have them yet, but he planned on having them soon after he got back to his ranch.

"Well, we're always interested in good mounts, but only good mounts, mind you.

"Sir, I can deliver to you fifty good horses in about four months from now." "Are they broken," asked the Major, "We don't have time to break horses." "No sir, but that won't be a problem. "How much do you want for these good horses," asked the Major. "What's the army willing to pay for good mounts," asked Monty. " Fifty-five dollars a horse," said the Major. "One hundred and fifty broken and delivered," said Monty. "One hundred," said the Major. "One hundred twenty sir, for prime broken horse flesh." "Done," said the Post Commander, and he held out his hand. As they shook on it, the Commander again emphasized, for good mounts already broken." True to his form Monty looked into the eyes of the General and asked, "May I have that in writing sir?" Surprised the Major looked at him and said, "Don't you trust the army, son?" "Yes Sir, but sometimes the army changes command and a whole post can change with it. "I see your point, All right." He wrote out an agreement and signed it Major Lee Van Housten. Monty put the agreement in his shirt pocket, shook hands with the Major and turned and left. He wanted to jump and shout but managed to keep himself composed as he walked toward his horse, Blackjack. The Commander, followed him to his horse was pleased when he saw the black Gelding. "Is this what I can expect," the Major asked? Monty mounted his horse and said to the major, "Close sir, close," and turned the black gelding and left the post.

    He caught up with the herd in the afternoon and everything was going as it should. He checked on Nathan and Shory and they said they felt they could ride now. "Give it one more day," said Monty. That night they circled the herd and down in a dry camp. In a distance they heard some wolves howling but they weren't close enough to consider them a threat.

    The next morning Running Bear came in pushing his mount as fast as it could go. He skidded to a stop close to Monty and said, "Whitemen ride this way. He held up his hands and showed all fingers twice." Monty whistled as loud as he could and signaled with his hat to stop the herd. Then he rode back to the riders and told them what Running Bear had said. They all pulled their weapons and checked their cylinders and magazines. "When do you think they will hit us, asked Red Barter? Monty looked at Running Bear who said, "Ambush near big rocks, indicated four miles ahead." Monty looked at his surroundings then said, "there's plenty of grass right here and there is a couple of run offs over there for water. That ought to hold them for a while. All right, Red, you and Tom stay with the herd, Zeke and Gague stay with the remuda. The rest of us will take the fight to them, said Monty. "The best defense is a good offense." We'll split up and circle wide around them and come on them from their backs. Again, show no mercy. These men mean to kill you and take from you what you have worked hard for almost three months to keep. They are too lazy and worthless to work hard like you. They are used to taking what they want, when they want. They have no regard for human life and no respect for the law. They respect only force and a gun. We're going to make our own law today. Someday it will be different but right now it isn't. Justice is up to us. When we find them, each of you pick out a man and fire when I do. And shoot to kill." "Now I know this may sound hard but they don't aim to take any prisoners, so we aren't either. They will shoot you in the back or between the eyes and laugh at you as you take your dying breath. They deserve no mercy and I don't plan to give them any. If any of you want to remain behind, I'll understand."

Not a man moved. Finally Sidney Meyers spoke up and said, "Boss, we all ride for the brand." Monty sat motionless for a moment, a feeling of pride and respect for each man. "All right, gentlemen let's ride," he said. and started Blackjackoff in the lead.

They rode slowly to keep their dust at a minimum. Running Bear led them behind some small hills, through some timber, and down some long draws. He put two fingers to his lips and motioned for them to be quiet. Each man got off his horse and took a hold of their horses' muzzle to keep them from whinnying to the outlaws horses. As they began to emerge on the side of a hill they saw some large boulders and large rocks scattered ahead. After circling them they ground hitched their mounts and Nathan stayed with the horses while the rest of them shucked their rifles and slipped their way toward the boulders and rocks. There were patches of sage and large cactus to hide behind as they advanced and encircled the waiting outlaws. Finally they eased far enough into the rocks and toping a knoll they saw the rustlers bedded down half way down the hill with their rifles pointing in the direction of the herd.

Running Bear was right, there were about twenty of them scattered in the rocks. One of them spoke loud enough to be herd, "something's wrong boss, we should be seeing the dust cloud by now." "Your right", said a man who was apparently their leader. He was a big man who wore a big black hat and a black kerchief tied around his neck. "Jack you and Patch go see if you can tell what's going on." Just then, Monty stood up, rifle in hand and pointed right at the their leader. "All right, raise your hands, you varmints, your covered, every one of you. Throw down…" He was interrupted by a bullet that glanced off the rock beside him. Monty squeezed his rifle trigger and the big man fell with his gun in hand. Monty then ducked behind a boulder and the rest of M/B riders began firing. Five of the rustlers fell down, not to get up again. The crew moved in closer firing as they moved. One bullet grazed Sidney's arm and another spat pieces of rock into the face of Mack Shorn. The near misses only made the M/B riders more angry and they pumped lead faster than ever. Then one of the outlaws jumped up to make a run for it, but he never got very far. He made three steps and started to jump behind a bolder but a bullet caught him mid-step and he crumbled and lay still. There was a lull in the fighting and Monty again yelled to the rustlers, "Your boss is dead and so are a lot of the rest of you. You want to fight this out to the last man or do you want get on your horses and ride out of here. After several minutes, they heard some horses running. Slowly they made their way forward. They saw the last of them mounting up and riding off as fast as they could. "I thought you said no mercy," said Short. "Your right, I did. But then I decided I didn't want to have to take the time to take them to a sheriff", said Monty. "Well, we could have hung them as cattle thieves," said Lefty." "I never thought of that", said Monty, "let's pick up what's left of their weapon and gun belts, then gather the horses left and go through their saddle bags. We'll take it all with us as usual".

They rode back to the herd and found every thing as should be. Shortbread tended to Sidney's flesh wound and put some salve on Mack's face where the rocks had cut through the skin. The next day they made fifteen miles and Monty had them to halt the cattle and bed them down. The next day he was riding into Abilene to see about selling the cattle. The next morning He and Lefty Gates rode into town. They stopped at the saloon, called "The Flying Mare" and went in and stepped up to the bar. They each ordered a beer and Monty told the bartender he had a herd bedded down outside of town and asked if there were any cattle buyers in town. The bartender nodded toward a gentleman sitting at a table about twenty feet away. Monty laid some extra money on the bar and said, "Thanks." Happily surprised the bartender grinned and picked up the money and said, "Anytime." Then he and Lefty made their way toward the cattle buyer. When they got to his table the man looked up at them. He was a well dressed man with a light colored suit and vest on. He was clean shaven of medium build. He looked to be in his forties and wore a typical Western hat. Monty introduced himself and told him that he had about twenty five hundred head of cattle for sale. He wondered if he was interested. He said he sure was interested but that was too many for him alone. However, he knew another buyer in town from Missouri and together they might take the whole herd. They agreed to meet that afternoon in the saloon. "By the way, My name is Mat Helmond of the Illinois Cattlemen's Association. Monty and Lefty shook hands with him and then excused themselves and went to find a restaurant. They each had a steak floating in grease, gravy, biscuits, potatoes, and coffee. Then they ordered apple pie. They sat there and enjoyed themselves until time to meet the cattle buyers. They walked back to the saloon and found both men were seated at a table. Monty and Lefty made their way and tipped their hats to them. Both men stood up and Mat Helmond introduced the other man as Henry Baxter of the Missouri Cattle Buyers Association. After a few words of light conversation Mat Helmond said they had talked it over, and if the stock met their approval they would pay top dollar for the cattle, since they were the first in. "What is top price," asked Monty? " Fifty dollars a head." "Sixty five, said Monty. We've spent too long on the trail and fought rustlers and Indians and storms to get these cattle here. If you don't want them, we'll hold them for another buyer. They will only get fatter." Mat Helmond laughed and said, "All right, sixty-five dollars a head." Monty reached out his hand and said, "deal." Each of them shook hands and Mat Helmond said to drive the cattle into the cattle bins and he would have a bank draft made out for the total amount. By the way just how large is this herd anyway. 1,857, we lost some along the way. "That's a lot of money," said the Missouri cattle buyer . "Yes, it is," said Monty, "and we worked hard for it."

"I'm sure you did" said the man from Illinois. With that they all shook hands and the buyers said, "We'll be at the bins by noon tomorrow."

They left the saloon and rode back to the herd. When he told the men the cattle had been sold they all yelled and threw their hats into the air. Shortbread went to his wagon brought out a couple of bottles and said, "I keep this for medicinal purposes, but I believe this is a night worth celebrating. The crew all stated their approval and reached for their cups.

The next morning they saddled up and Tom, Red, and Zeek staying behind to watch the remainder of the horse herd. The rest of the horses taken from the indians and outlaws were herded along with the cattle to town. Shortbread said he preferred to stay with his wagon. Running Bear wanted nothing to do with the "Whiteman's town."

The men drove the cattle into the cattle bins and Gage and Curley stayed with the herd while the rest of them rode in and stopped at the sheriff's office. Monty went in and introduced himself and stated he was selling his cattle to two cattle buyers. News like this travels fast. "Is there anyone in particular I need to watch out for," asked Monty.

The sheriff looked at him said, "there are always those around you need to watch out for. Are you the gents that worked over those rustlers the other night? The word around is that you're a pretty salty bunch and 'crack shots.'" Monty nodded his head and said, "Well, we had some trouble but nothing we couldn't handle."

The sheriff nodded and got up and walked with the M/B riders down to the saloon. Hellman and Baxter were there. They got up and they all went down to the cattle bins. They looked over the stock and agreed they were of the finest herds they had seen. Top dollar it was. They took their tally and found it agreed with Monty's with a few over. Each of them made out a bank draft the amount totaling, One hundred twenty, two hundred fifty thousand dollars. Monty thanked them and went straight to the bank. He presented the drafts to the teller and wanted to know if they were good for the amount. A few moments later he returned and said they were good. Monty thanked him and he and his crew headed for their horses and rode back to camp.

Monty had picked up a couple bottles of refreshment and took it back to the crew to celebrate that night. Although they knew they couldn't celebrate too heavily because they knew someone might want to try and take that money away from them. And if they did, they wanted to be ready. They were right of course. That night, in the early morning hours, eight riders slipped their horses toward the camp. The camp fire had just been refueled and was burning strong. Its light showed the blankets of the crew. All appeared to be asleep. One of the would be thieves whispered. "Now" and they let loose with a barrage of bullets striking all the beds they could see. The firing lasted for several seconds. Then the firing ended and all was still. Not a sound. Only a lot of blue smoke drifted in the light breeze. The ambushers walked toward the riddled beds.

Suddenly a voice off to their right sounded. It was Monty's voice. "All right, your covered from two sides. Drop your guns or we'll kill you all. Drop them now!" "I'll be blamed if I will," said one of the thieves and slung a shot in Monty's direction. Monty and the whole M/B riders opened up at the same time.

The outlaws were outlined by the fire light and five of the eight fell down. The three others started to run but they too never got past two steps. "Hold it," yelled Monty. Slowly the drovers came out of the darkness still pointing their guns in the direction of the outlaws. A few were moaning but most were beyond making any noise. Monty's crew did the best they could for those wounded. Later that morning Monty, Gague, Red, Short, and Mack saddled up and took the dead, the wounded, and those lucky enough to still be alive, into town. Monty had the cashier's check tucked inside a money belt and it was around his middle, underneath his shirt. He stopped at the sheriff's office and told him what had happened and that he had taken their guns and would take their horses if the sheriff didn't object. The rest stopped in front of the local tavern and walked in together. It was fairly empty with about ten men scattered around in the saloon. As they stepped up to the bar Monty told the bartender to serve each of the M/b riders 3 rounds of what ever they wanted. He would pay the tab.

As the bartender poured Monty his drink he said in low tones for him to watch his back because word had circulated around that he was carrying around a large amount of cash and that there had been some pretty rough customers that over heard it. Monty thanked him. He also told the bartender of the attempted robbery the previous night. He told his riders they could go over to the general store if they needed anything and he would pick up their tab against their wages. They all agreed. Then he looked at each of them as he said they were not to engage in any poker games and not to get into any trouble. They wanted to leave town in two hours and head back to camp. They all shook their heads in agreement. He told them he would be at the sheriff's office.

About an hour later Short came running into the sheriff's office and said to Monty, "Boss, you better come quick Sidney's about to get himself killed."

Monty jumped up and took off running, the sheriff and Short running behind him. When Monty reached the saloon he pulled his iron out and bolted into the saloon. The Sheriff and Short were about ten feet behind him.

He found Sidney surrounded by four men, one with his gun drawn. Then he saw five other men with their guns drawn pointed at the rest of the H/B riders. The man with the gun held on Sidney turned to look at Monty who never stopped moving but fired his gun at the gun hand of the man covering Sidney. The blast caught the man's pistol and the bullet turned and went up his forearm. He yelled and jerked his arm toward his side, blood immediately spurting on his shirt and the floor. Monty then pointed his gun toward the rest of the men and asked in an angry voice, "whose next? Just make a move and we'll see who comes out on top." They all froze. The sheriff spoke up, "What's going on here?" Nathan spoke up first, "Sidney was kissing a girl over there and this man didn't like it. He said she was his girl. The girl told him she was nobody's girl and to leave her alone. "Sidney told the man to mind his own business. He told the rest of these men that we drovers needed to be taught a lesson. We remembered what you said boss, about no trouble so they got the drop on us. This man you shot was trying to get Sidney to draw on him. When he refused he called him yellow and drew his gun and that's when you came in. I think if you hadn't he would have killed Sidney, just because he kissed that girl. If she was his girl".

Monty turned to the sheriff and said, "All right sheriff, do you want to take it from here or shall we have a shoot out." The sheriff didn't like Monty's remark and told him to put up his gun. He was sheriff here and he would keep the peace without his help. Monty holstered his gun as did everyone else. Two men got a hold of the wounded man and they took him to see the doctor. The sheriff turned to Monty and said, "Mr. Lane, I think it best if you took your men and left town now. That way there won't be any further trouble here." Monty looked at his men and asked, "What about it men, you ready to leave this town?" They all agreed, and they walked out side and mounted , backed up their horses and then rode unmolested out of town and back to camp.

When they got back to camp Sidney told Monty he was sorry to have caused so much trouble. Monty told him to not give it any more thought. One thing came out of it. They were a tough crew and it might discourage any further trouble from anyone in town.

Shortbread fixed their supper and they turned in, glad there was no herd to guard, except the remuda. Monty had sold a number of the outlaw's horses they had accumulated and the indian ponies. Some of the riders still had their extra horses.

Monty posted guards for the night anyway. It was a restful and peaceful night.

Chapter Twelve

They rose early the next morning and since they had no cattle to drive they made thirty-five miles the first day. When they got near the army post Monty suggested they stop and the men could go to the dry goods store if they wanted to. They arrived at the fort and Monty gave each of them all of the money they had taken from the outlaws along with the money he had gotten for selling their horses and guns. That was a bonus they hadn't expected. When they reached the fort the men quickly went to the post store. Red bought a red flannel shirt (what other color) and some socks. Short bought a new hat, Lefty a pair of jeans, and Mack bought a Bowie knife. Soon after that they were on their way home again and things went well for them with no trouble along the trail.

When they approached Monty's ranch he told them to put their horses in the corral. Then he said he was going over to the Circle B. He had business to attend to.

They men laughed as they watched the Brown raise a cloud of dust. The black trailed after them. Monty rode the Brown at a stiff pace until he was in sight of the ranch. He rode up to the corral and unsaddled his horse. Just then Nathan came out of the barn carrying a saddle. He saw Monty, dropped the saddle, and ran to meet him. The two men shook hands firmly. It was good to see one another again. Then Monty told Nathan his reason for this drive and why it was so important to him. Nathan already knew this. Monty said, "Nathan, you're the nearest thing to a father that Beth has. I want your permission to marry her." Nathan grinned big and stuck out his right hand and said, "I am proud to say yes. Beth couldn't find a better man than yourself." "Thanks Nathan, I'll try to be worthy of her." Nathan grinned at him and said, "Beth already told me about your proposal." We're all happy for both of you. "Thanks," said Monty as he headed toward the big house. Monty then walked up and knocked on the door. Beth opened the door and squealed with delight as she saw Monty standing there. She flung her arms around his neck and hugged him so tightly that Monty almost lost his balance. He stepped inside and hugged her again. Then for the first time he leaned his head forward toward hers and she lifted her lips toward his and then in a strong embrace their lips met and lingered for a long time. As they released their embrace Monty said to her, "Beth, he said, "I've wanted to do that since the first day I saw you." Again they hugged one another. Then stepping back a step he said to her, "Beth the trail drive was a success. Do you still want me? I want you to be my wife." Bethany's eyes filled with tears and she said, "Oh Monty, why wouldn't I still want you? I love you. I love you with all my heart and I always will." Then she broke out into tears and held him close. After a few seconds he took her by the hand and asked her to sit down. Then he told her about his plans for his ranch and how he dreamed to stock it with good brood mares and to sell horses. He told her about the contract he already had with the Army. She listened to him and then asked, "when do we plan to get married?" " How about around six months from now?" "That long?" she asked. "The time will pass quickly, he said. "Maybe for you, but not for me, Monty Lane! That sounds like a lifetime away!" "Where will we live, your ranch or mine, or do you plan for us to live at separate ranches," she teased. I think we should live here, he said. My crew will live at my ranch and work it for me. That way I can travel back and forth as needed. I'm calling it the M/B ranch, with your permission. That way we both will have an interest in it. She smiled at him and hugged and kissed him again. The next day Monty and Beth rode into town and went to the bank and deposited his cashier's check. He then had the banker to transfer the amount of Beth's cattle money to her account. She started to protest but he insisted it be done this way. He then payed off his mortgage on the ranch and withdrew enough to pay his crew.

When he rode back to the M/B ranch he and Beth met with his crew and paid them for the drive with each man getting a $100 bonus. Then he asked how many of them wanted to remain as riders for the M/B? Their pay will be forty-five dollars a month, food and board provided. Most of them said they wanted to stay with him. Shortbread sort of hung back, not saying much. He was slowly walking with drooped shoulders toward his mules and wagon. Monty looked at him and said, "Shortbread, after we round up our brood mares will you be ready to "hang up" that wagon of yours? We sure do need a cook." Shortbread turned around and looked at Monty and asked, "You really mean that Mr. Monty?" "Yes we do shortbread." said Bethany. "She's right" said Monty. "Well, it was all right having a colored man as a cook on the trail. But we're home now and that sometimes makes a difference to folks." "Not to us, does it men?" They all joined in patting Shortbread on the arms, shoulders, and back saying they wanted him to stay. "Well," he said, "I guess I ain't got nowhere else to go. I believe I'll just stay then." "Hurray," they all shouted together. "What about my mules and my wagon," asked Shortbread? "Well for the time being put your wagon over in that shed and turn your mules out in the southwest pasture" said Monty. "Their yours to keep, sell, or trade, after we're done with them," said Monty. Shortbread started walking over to the team and was mumbling to them, "You hear that mules, we got us a home here as long as we want. I declare... I do declare." Running Bear had not returned with them, but had gone back to his own people.

Monty knew he must take time to go and see Running Bear and thank him for all of his help and guidance.

Monty told the men of his dream of building a horse ranch. He told them how he planned to start it by catching wild horses and culling them, keeping the best ones for brood mares, and to sort out the yearlings and such. He would let the rest return to the plains. That way there would always be plenty to replenish the herds still roaming the plains. "Some day that time is going to end. But I want to keep it going as long as I can."

Later he also told them about his army contract. Their first job was to mend the fences that had been allowed to fall down during the roundup. Then they were to divide the north range into two sections and the same with the land west of the ranch. Another project was to rebuild the bunkhouse that Monty had partly destroyed with the dynamite. A not so popular project was to clean the springs and the creeks that flowed through the ranch and those close by. They must build a reservoir for possible droughts.

After working long hard days for a couple of months they finally came to the place where they were ready to trap the wild mustangs that roamed the plains.

Monty and his crew searched the hills for the mustangs. Several herds were sighted. Then it was a matter of studying the habits of the herds and glassing them to see which ones he wanted first. They went to work digging post holes, cutting saplings, moving brush until they had a large brush corral built near a canyon. They took their time doing this so it could become a part of the terrain. They blocked the back of the canyon that had a narrow outlet. The front of the canyon lay open to the surrounding hills. Finally they were finished. Monty decided on a herd that frequented a waterhole not far from where they had built the brush corral. Their presence had become familiar to the mustangs. Then the day of trapping the mustangs was at hand. They circled the herd until they could head them in the right direction. This was a herd that had at least ten good mares that he would use as brood mares. There were some good looking colts and yearlings and a number of other horses that could be used toward the army contract.

Early the next morning the horses had come to the water hole to drink. They had only been there a few minutes when suddenly Monty and the M/B riders appeared fanning out and waving their hats, yelling as loud as they could. It worked. The horses started toward the brush corral. The riders fanned out farther gaining on the herd. Just before the lead horse got to the entrance of the corral, it started to shy to one side but Lefty Gates closed in from that side waving his lariat. The lead mare went through the corral entrance and the rest followed, including the stallion. The corral was plenty deep and wide. Some of the horses were crashing against the brush trying to get through. So far it was holding. On both sides of the fence were rock walls that were too sheer to climb and there were no spaces wide enough for the horses to get through.

The M/B riders then began working to block the entrance of the brush coral. It was several hours before they finished. They looked over the mustangs. There were all colors but mostly blacks and browns. There were a few paints, buckskins, several roan, chestnuts, and a couple of palominos. The stallion was a large white horse whose pinkish hide showed the signs of numerous battle scars. He kept pacing up and down the brush fence, his brown eyes trying to find a weakness. Finding none he went to the other side and tried to climb the boulders but they were just too steep. He would get a few feet and then slide back down. Monty rode Blackjack in with a lariat in his hand. The horses moved away but Monty just kept walking the black following slowly. He spotted a roan mare that he liked and spurred Blackjack who bolted toward the mare. She whirled to run but it was too late. The rope settled around her neck and she reared and snorted loudly. She squealed and violently shook her head and voiced her protest. Again she reared but Monty had his rope cinched to his saddle. This time when she came down he began backing Blackjack slowly. He pulled the mare toward a tall tree. She whinnied in protest and kicked out her back feet but she followed Blackjack's strong pull. Monty double cinched the rope around the tree securing it. Lefty came in and did the same as Monty was roping a chestnut. Each of the cowboys took their turns roping a mare that Monty pointed out and tying them to a sapling or a boulder. After the ten mares were selected and secured, Monty pointed out ten yearlings that appealed to him and they were roped and secured also. Then they herded some of the culls toward the front of the makeshift corral and took down the gates and drove them out, including the white stallion. They continued their flight to freedom until they were well out of sight. The gates were then put back in place.

That evening as they crew had nearly finished working for the day, one of the riders came to Monty and told him he had seen a couple of riders sitting on a hill off to the north watching them. He also said that later in the day he noticed four riders watching them. They never offered to get any closer, they just kept watching. The M/B rider asked him what he made of it? Monty stood there thoughtfully for a minute then said, "I don't know, but we'll keep our attention on it. Right now let's keep on doing what we're doing with this herd. It could be that they're "herd cutters." But we don't have enough horses to merit herd cutters. Nevertheless we need to be ready for them. Spread the word among the crew about this and when they come in we'll be ready."

"What if they wait until we bunk down for the night?" Monty grinned and said, "We have a plan for that too." With that they spread out and continued their work but quietly let the word drift among the outfit letting them know what was about to take place.

It was about two hours later that three riders approached the M/B hands. One of them said to two of the hands branding the horses they were going to keep, "We would like to talk to your boss about a job. Can you point him out to me?"

The hand with the smoking branding iron in his hand pointed to another nearby cowboy sitting in his saddle watching the branding of a buckskin mare. That's him on that black gelding." "Thanks" replied the man. The three then rode to Monty. Monty saw them coming but never turned toward them. He figured he already knew what this was about.

In Pursuit of a Dream | 91

"Excuse us mister, we were told you were the boss. We'd like a word with you if you can spare a minute? Monte turned toward them and stepped down off his horse and said, "I'm listening."

"Well," said the stranger, we just wanted you to know that some where in the next few minutes you're going to be hit by a large number of riders needing some horses. Now they don't want to take all of them, just say about a dozen or so, and I'm sure these fellers will be satisfied. There won't be any gun fire and nobody will get hurt. Now what do you say? And remember there are about twenty to twenty-five of us."

Suddenly there was a six gun in Monty's hand. It appeared from nowhere, and it was shoved against the outlaw's side. In a low voice Monty said to the would be rustler, "Mister, I'm only going to say this once so listen closely. And remember your life depends on it, so listen and remember it well. You tell that "loser of a boss" of yours that they're not getting even one of these horses. We worked too hard to collect them. And if you try to take them we'll fight you to the last man. Our aim will be to kill you with no mercy given. We'll chase you clean out of the state if we have to. But you aren't getting one horse from us without a fight. All I have to do is fire one shot and the war is on, you got that Mister"? "One shot!"

"Yes sir." "Please don't shoot. I'm just a delivery man. "That's right, Mister Delivery Man. Now you just deliver that message to your boss and you might live to see another day. Now get!" Monty slowly lowered his gun and holstered it. The three would be rustlers kicked their heels into their horses' flanks and never looked back. "Boss, you must have made a good case because they lit out of here like their horses tails were on fire." One of Monty's riders said to him, "Monty, where did you have that gun, I didn't see you draw it?" "It was in it's holster where it belonged," said Monty. The rest of the night went peaceably with no interruptions.

That evening Shortbread showed up with his chuck wagon and fixed a good meal of beef, beans, cornbread, biscuits and coffee…and apple pie. The crew showed their appreciation by eating it all up. Nothing went to waste.

The next morning Monty went to his roan, talking to her in low gentle tones. As he slowly walked toward her tense body he could see that she was all tensed up and he knew the tone of his voice was important. It didn't matter what he said as much as how he said it. Softly, slowly, each step! The mare reared several times. He would stop until she came down and then continue walking slowly towards the roan. The rope was very tight around her neck. She was learning that pulling away hurt and was useless. Finally Monty reached the horse's head and securely took hold of the rope where it went around her neck. Lefty eased toward him with a hackamore behind him. When he came around on the other side of her and while Monty held the horse Lefty put the hackamore on her. Monty then slowly loosened the rope around her neck and worked it through the hackamore while Nathan held her head down. Monty then tied his rope to the hackamore, loosened the end around the post. The mare trembled at his touch and stomped her front hoof. Monty continued to talk softly to her. He led her around a bit talking to her as they walked again stopping and petting her neck. Ever so often he would stop and put his arm over her neck and put his weight across her back. After a time of leading her around the corral he stopped and slowly let her smell the saddle blanket… when she would pull away he would start over. The same with the saddle, until she offered no resistance. As he continued to talk slowly and softly to her he stepped into the left stirrup. He didn't throw his leg over, he just let her feel his weight…finally he slowly threw his leg over and rested easy in the saddle. He slowly learned forward just a bit and rubbed her neck. Then still speaking softly to her he dismounted. As he continued to speak to her he rubbed her shoulders, her neck, her head, her side, and then her hips. Then he would begin the process all over again. Then he would let the horse rest for about an hour while he worked with another horse, then he would begin the process over again.

Monty mounted the Roan. She bucked straight up and then jumped sideways and squealed her displeasure, but he continued until she slowly began to settled down and began to walk. She was still jittery, nervous, and unsure of this rider but she couldn't throw him off. This was repeated until she finally accepted him.

Each cowboy took his turn working a hackamore on the horse they had roped and leading the horse until it decided it was O.K. to be roped and led. . They didn't work with the yearlings. They would take them back to the ranch and let them mature. It was a long hard day and Shortbread fixed an evening meal that caused them to forget the struggles of the day. The next morning they mounted and took their horses and rode to the watering hole and allowed the horses to drink their fill. Monty went first, leading his new horse into deeper water. She reared in resistance but then followed. He kept making the distance shorter between them until Blackjack was beside the mare. Both horses were up to their bellies in the water and Monty slid from Blackjack on to the roan mare. She tried to rear but couldn't put up much of a fight. Monty stayed with her pulling her head to one side, forcing her to go in circles instead of running out of the water. When she was tired and stopped bucking he allowed her to move toward the bank. She tried to buck several times but the fight had gone out of her. Oh, she would protest for a while but the main battle was over. Monty held tightly to the hackamore and dismounted. Blackjack was right there beside him as he had been trained.

The rest of the crew worked their horses the same way until they were ready to return to the ranch. Then they tied four horses together with two cowboys holding a rope on the lead horse. Then four more followed, then two. They did the same with the yearlings. As they headed for the ranch the riders that were free rode as flank riders.

They reached the ranch that evening and turned the mares loose in a strongly built corral with a high fence. Then they took their own mounts and unsaddled them, rubbed them down good and put them in the large barn. The horses were watered and fed.

The next day they cut tall grass and carried it out to the corral and water was poured into a large water trough. The men all went in to the bunk house and laid down on their beds. They were tired. Very tired! But each man was pleased with himself and the work he had done that day.

Two days later Monty's day was interrupted by an unwelcome voice. He recognized it immediately, Vicky! It was too late to dash out of sight. He turned and saw her and Beth walking toward him. Beth had a crocked grin on her face.

Vicki had a smile on hers that stretched from "ear to ear." "How are you Monty?"

"Well, right now I'm pretty busy," he answered. She rather ignored his comment and went right on with her conversation. "Beth tells me you are preparing to go out and catch some more mustangs. That right?" Monty didn't answer but just nodded. "Well I won't keep you. I just wanted to see you again. Remember, I'll be thinking about you. I do that all the time anyway." Monty kind of grunted, then he turned and walked over to Bethany and reached down and took her in his arms and kissed her. Vicky grinned and asked, "What about me cowboy, do I get one of those?" Monty turned toward his horse as he said, "Sorry, I'm fresh out." When he settled in his saddle, Vicky, grinning, said to him, "I can wait until you get back." Monty touched three of his fingers to his "Stetson" and turned Blackjack and headed out. As Beth and Vicky walked back toward the house Beth said to her visiting friend,

"Vicky, do you know Monty and I are to be married, not long from now?" Without looking at her, Vicky answered, "yes, I heard that."

"Well, why do you persist in chasing him?" Vicky looked at Beth with a smile on her face and said, "Well, a girl can dream can't she? He's a very handsome man!"

"But it's hopeless for you Vicky." Vicky turned her head toward Beth and said, "Well, maybe so …and again, maybe not, you never know." Beth stopped and looked at Vicky, who also stopped. The two women stood there looking at one another for a long moment and then Beth said, "He's mine Vicky, all mine. He's asked me to marry him when he returns from this drive, and I've said, "yes." Vicky only smiled and said, "You never know, Beth, you just never know."

Beth then said to her, "Vicky, I don't want you to come here any more. I know we've been good friends for a long time but you're pushing things too far. Monty hasn't appreciated your remarks and the suggestions you've made. I think it would be better if you didn't come around until after the wedding."

Vicky, smiled, and asked, "What's the matter Beth, afraid of a little competition?"

Beth answered, "No, Vicky, I just don't want to lose your friendship."

Vicky smiled and said, "O.K. If that's the way you want it, I won't return. You don't mind if I attend the wedding do you'? "Well, of course not, you're invited to the wedding, if you want to come," said Beth. Neither of them said anymore until they arrived at the ranch and Vicky mounted her horse and rode away, without a wave of the hand or a "goodby." Monty led the M/B riders back out on the prairie. He left Mack Shears and Red Barter at the ranch to keep watch and tend to the new mares. Monty sent Tom Wells and Curley Springs out as scouts. Shortbread had brought his chuck wagon and prepared meals for the men again. After two days Curley and Tom returned with reports of two different herds near enough to be driven into the brush coral. The next day Monty rode with them and glassed both herds. He selected the one that was led by a big Red stallion. He guessed there were about nine mares well worth keeping and a number of colts and yearlings. Monty said aloud, "That sure is a good looking stallion. He's about the best I've seen out on the plains."

There were horses of all colors in the herd. Many were solid colors and some where spotted. Several of the colts were frolicking chasing one another. There were a couple lying on the ground sleeping, taking in the warm sun. And a few were getting their dinner. The stallion was standing on a short knoll looking after his herd. Ever once in a while he would test the air for smells and his ears twitched in different directions always watching and listening for danger. The riders would use the same plan as before, waiting until the horses were at a watering hole and then rushing out making as much noise as they could fanning out as far as they dared and keeping the herd headed in the direction they wanted them to go. As they began the chase after them, again the herd ran through the corral entrance and realized too late that it was a trap. The red stallion raced to the front of the herd and reared high and whistled his rage trying to turn his herd but it was too late. By the time they reversed themselves and started back the M/B riders were inside with the gates in place. Some of the horses crashed against the coral fence and it withstood their punishment. The riders raised their hats into the air and shouted at the herd as they thundered their way within the trap corral. Their presence and noise was enough to turn the herd back again and head them away from the coral brush fence. They spent most of the day watching the horses. They drank their fill of water from a small spring within the corral. The stallion was restless. He kept trying to find a way out, but there were no holes in the corral and the walls were just too steep. Then he turned and ran right at his enemies that had pursued him and had driven his herd into this trap. The riders stood their ground, but his determination drove him on. At the last minuted they spurred their horses out of the way for fear he would crash into them. Instead he did the unbelievable. When he reached the corral he leaped with all of his strength and cunning and cleared a lower spot in the brush corral. There wasn't a rider there that thought that he could have cleared it. When the gallant stallion landed on the other side of the fence he stumbled and went to his knees, but he quickly regained his footing and reared high with his forelegs flailing the air in defiance of his enemies and then he was off at a dead run. He was free! Monty quickly removed two bars from the corral and shouted at Lefty and Nathan to follow him. Their horses jumped the lowered gate and were in hot pursuit of the big red stallion. Monty was on Blackjack running as fast as his horse could run. Lefty wondered why he let the other stallion go and wanted this one but he followed orders. The red stallion was fast and Blackjack was trying hard to keep up. He wasn't gaining but he was keeping the stallion in sight. That was all that mattered right now. Monty wished he was riding the Brown but he knew that wouldn't work once he caught up with the stallion. There would be a challenge and a fight to the death. Monty slowed the black to conserve his strength. They followed the red horse for miles. He was tiring but also trying to dodge them with his cunning. Twice they lost his tracks but Lefty was a tracker. He could trail a snake across a barren rock. Then skylined on a high ridge they spotted the stallion, who also was watching them. They slowed their horses to a trot to give them some rest. When they were a half mile away the stallion disappeared on the other side. Monty motioned for them to split around the ridge and meet on the other side. When they met around on the other side the red was no where in sight and there were three long draws in which he could have taken. Lefty dismounted and studied the ground carefully, then he mounted his horse and started off on the draw farthest to the left. Unknown to the red stallion it led to a dead end with steep banks and large boulders. The red stallion was trapped, and he knew it. He kept pacing and looking for a way out. When Monty, Nathan. and Lefty appeared the stallion reared high with his forelegs slashing the air. He screamed at them and charged, then stopped after about twenty feet. He shook his head violently at them and lashed out at them with his right foreleg. He beared his teeth with open mouth warning them not to come any closer. All three riders stopped and took out their lariats uncoiling them. Slowly they approached the red stallion as he stood motionless for about ten seconds then he bolted toward them at full charge with his ears laid back.

Monty and Lefty were about twenty feet apart and the stallion headed for the middle of that distance. As he passed between them both men shot out their loops. Monty turned his black at the same time and skidded to a halt. His rope neatly settled around the red stallion's neck and then Monty spurred his black in the direction of the fleeing stallion so when he hit the end of the rope it wouldn't pull Blackjack off his feet. Lefty had missed and was recoiling his rope for another toss. The Red hit the end of the rope and was brought up short. He reared and fought against it. Lefty and Nathan quickly got into position and Lefty threw a loop over the stallion and secured it to his saddle. The red horse reared and bucked pulling against the ropes until it almost cut his wind off. Finally his resistance began to sap his strength and slowly he quieted down and breathing hard he stood looking at them defiantly. Slowly they moved their horses back toward the way they had come. After a few moments the red again bolted between them and that was what they were waiting for. They took in their slack and he was held tight between them making it easier to lead. They kept their distance from him because once in a while he would get a new urge to fight and lash out with a kick.

It was evening before they arrived back at camp. The crew had already caught and post-tied five of the mares that Monty had pointed out. Curley Springs, who was a good horseman, had also selected two more he thought Monty might like. He guessed right. They led the stallion to a sizable tree and tied both ropes to it.

All the riders gathered around the stallion, at a safe distance, and admired the horse. He was about as fine an animal as they would find on the plains, or anywhere else. He stood 15 to 15 1/2 hands high. His coat color was a distinct red color with a little darker color of his mane and tail. His head was smaller than some but his neck was quite muscular. Lefty whistled as he looked at the Red's hindquarters. They looked quite muscular and solid. Lefty commented to Curley, "Man those hindquarters are pure muscle machines." Big Red had settled down as they all admired him. They all wondered where he came from. It was apparent that there was some good bloodlines in his past. Then they turned their attention to the rest of the herd and caught ten more mares and twelve yearlings. They worked them the same way they did the other herd. They were thankful that Shortbread was there to keep them fed. They were tired and very hungry. It only took a few riders to keep watch at night since they were corralled. During the day they worked and worked with the horses trying to get them used to the ropes and that it was useless to fight against them. Finally they were ready for the water lessons. There was a spring the ran through the canyon and it was about four to five foot in some places, especially where the banks sloped slightly downward. Each man worked the mares as before and finally after a couple more days they had the horses to where they could be ridden in the shallow water. Monty and Lefty worked with the red stallion. Each time Monty tried to ride the stallion in the water he had Lefty to keep his rope on him. The stallion was a fighter and refused to give in. After three days Monty had made little progress. He spent time each day talking to the stallion, taking him to water. However, he was not yet able to touch his neck or head. Finally, on the fourth day as he approached the red stallion it backed off to the end of the rope but did not fight. Monty had pulled some sweet grass and was holding it out to him. When he was close enough the big horse stretched his neck toward him as far as he could. He smelled of the grass and snorted. Monty stood still. A second and third time he smelled of the grass and jerked back his head. Finally he nibbled at the grass still in Monty's hand. After a couple times of this Monty led the horse to a tree and tied him where there was nothing to eat or drink. Twice more in the day he approached the horse with something to eat and then took a long lead rope and hooked it to the halter. He rubbed his hand slowly against the horse's body, his head, his hips, and then he would gently flip the rope where it landed on the red horse's back. He skidded away from it. Monty again flipped it to his back. Again he skidded away from it. Then Monty let it fall on the top of his hips, and he shook it off. Several times he flipped the rope and let it fall of his back hip and then he would shake it off. Monty continued this until the red stallion allowed it rope to rest on either of his back hips. then he lightly bounced it against his hips and let it fall on its lower legs. Then its back again. Monty worked the rope up and down his mane. For a long time he kept talking, flipping, and rubbing the red horse. Finally he could see that the stallion had accepted it. He did that several times that day. Then, next day he took a saddle blanket and did the same thing, getting the horse used to the blanket. Finally, he could put the saddle blanket across the stallion's back and he did not resist. He stiffened for a minute and then slowly relaxed.

Now came the hard part…the saddle. This might be a long process. He held the saddle in front of the stallion allowing him to see it, to let his nose smell of it.

Sometimes he would lead the Stallion away from it, but then lead him back to it and allow him to smell of it, or put his nose against it.

Finally came the day, after seeing it, smelling of it, allowing it to touch his side … Monty lifted it up and as gently as he could, he set the saddle on the horse's back.

That set him back to tensing up again. Monty spent most of the day aquatinting the big red horse with the saddle. He then took it to his side and as he lifted it, the stallion swung his hips away from the saddle. Monty kept saying, "easy boy, easy." He walked around in front of the horse and let him smell of it again. After he had smelled of it several times he walked around again to his left side. Monty slowly laid his arm across the horse's back. He put some of his weight across the horse's back. Finally, he gently placed the saddle on the horse's back. He flinched but didn't attempt to buck it off. Slowly Monty secured it to the horse, talking to it all the time. After it was securely on, it was easy to see that the red stallion was not sure about this whole thing, but he was permitting it. Then he slowly began to lead the red stallion around the corral. He unsaddled the stallion, he now called Red, and let him rest. But after a bit Monty was at it again. Round and round the corral. The cinch was tight, every thing was as it should be, except Monty in the saddle. Finally, Monty decided it was time! He had been leaning on the horses' saddle from time to time. It was now or never. He put his foot in the stirrup and swung his leg over. He landed smoothly in the saddle. He felt the Red stiffen and he immediately began talking to him. He placed his hand on Red's neck and talked to him. He then dismounted and rubbed his hand over his neck, his shoulders, and his hips . Then when he felt the Red horse had relaxed he would mount up again. He kept doing this until he could mount the Stallion and he showed no sign of stiffening up. He called to Lefty and told him to come and lead the Red stallion around with Monty in the saddle. After several rounds of this, Monty told Lefty to take down the corral gate poles to let him out. Lefty turned his head and looked at Monty and asked, "You sure you want to do this boss?" Monty said, "I do." With this done Monty guided the The Red Stallion out of the corral and then stopped as Monty pulled back gently on the bit. As Lefty replaced the coral poles Monty said, "Here goes nothing and with that he gently touched his spurs to the horse's flanks and off they went.

Lefty yelled, "Ridem cowboy!!!" At Monty's encouragement, the Red Stallion reared high on his back legs and when he landed he did not buck but began to run. He began to "pick'em up and lay them down." Monty guided him towards the plains where he encouraged him to run faster still…finally he was running all out, running to the country from whence he had come. Monty let him run as fast as he wanted to. He pulled his hat down on his head so he wouldn't lose it. He attempted to turn the Red stallion to a different direction. No problem, he guided with little prompting. Monty wondered who had trained him before? Or was this just a natural for him.

Monty let him run until the red stallion began to slow down on his own. Then he guided him back to the herd and the corral. Monty was jubilant with the Red Stallion's performance. He unsaddled him and rubbed him down.

Then he looked squarely into the red stallion face and said, "I'm quitting while I'm ahead." With that he reached up an rubbed his hand over the stallions neck and patted it. Then he quickly exited to the outside of the corral. Once out he looked at Lefty and said, "man that took it out of me. I didn't know what to expect."

Several hours later Monty again approached the Red Stallion and went through the process of saddling him. This time it was an easier process but with some tense moments. After he was saddled Monty took the reins and slowly put his foot into the stirrup. He talked to the horse as he tested his weight in the stirrup. The stallion stiffened. Monty stepped back out of the stirrup, he talked to the horse and patted its neck. Again he tried to step into the stirrup. He repeated this until finally the horse permitted him to swing his leg over the saddle. He reared up and whinnied but then came back down as Monty kept talking to him and patted his neck. He also had a hand full of mane. When the stallion came back down he did not kick out his hind feet. Rather, he just stood there motionless. Monty got off and praised the animal and talked to him as he patted and rubbed his neck. He mounted again and again. Finally, he very lightly touched his heel to the horse's side and urged it forward. It did so, but Monty could feel its tenseness. He knew any sudden or wrong move could cause another explosion of bucking. After mounting and walking him around a bit with no resistance Monty touched his side again and the stallion began to run faster. He continued to run in the corral until the horse was running from one end of the big corral to the other. Finally, he dismounted and opened the corral gates and rode the big red horse out into the open range. Monty motioned for one of the hands standing their to replace the gate poles. He sat there a minute waiting to see the Red's reaction. He acted no different. Monty urged him to go and then let him run. The stallion was not running all out but he was running at a fast pace causing the wind to rush against Monty's face. He pulled down the brim of his hat closer on his head and encouraged the stallion run until he began to slow down on his own. Then he rode him back to the corral and whistled to Blackjack to come and he followed. The red stallion had to learn to tolerate Blackjack. He was no threat to the Red Stallion in any way.

It was time to break camp and head back to the Circle B. They gathered their stock together, and Shortbread followed with his wagon. Monty rode the red stallion back to the Circle B. He knew he could not take him to the M/B where his big Brown Stallion was. The two could never be put close together. They were both wild herd stallions. Each had been the master of his own herd and one would not tolerate the other.

When Monty rode into the Circle B ranch the stallion smelled his own herd before he saw them in the large corral. He called to them and some of them answered. The ranch hands that were there had heard of the big horse and they stayed at a safe distance so they would not frighten him. Monty rode the stallion into the corral and tied him to a hitching post, remembering how high this horse could jump. Monty went toward the big house and Beth came running toward him. She threw her arms around him and hugged him tightly and told him how glad she was to see him. Nathan came out of the barn and saw the big red stallion. He whistled and walked to the corral. "Man that is some horse," he said. Monty and Beth joined him. Monty said, "Nathan, I'm going to have two horse herds. One will be the Browns and the other will be this big Red Fella. I'll have the best horses in the country. Beth held his arm tightly and she could feel the excitement in his voice. In her own mind she could sense his dream. If this was his dream, it would be her dream too. He was her man!

A week later Monty remembered Running Bear and decided that with Beth's permission he would take twenty steers and leave them with the tribe in appreciation of Running Bear's service to them. He also took warm blankets, knives, tobacco, rifles, and ammunition, along with twelve good horses. They rounded up the steers and horses and started for Running Bear's village.

Lefty and Nathan went with him. They rode to where they had met the Indians and tried to follow the directions that Running Bear had given to him. They rode in that direction and hoped the tribe would still be there.. They camped close to where they thought the village might be. The next day about noon suddenly three Indians appeared on a hillside riding toward them. Running Bear was in the lead. He rode toward Monty, who had a big grin on his face, dismounted and waited for them to come to him. Running Bear raised his hand in friendship. Their chief was with them and Monty remembered he spoke English, as well as Running Bear. Monty raised his arm to the Chief. The chief raised his arm in return. Monty pointed toward Lefty and said, "friend." The chief nodded and Lefty returned in like manner. Then Monty turned and looked at Beth beside him and pointed to her and said, "Squaw!" Running Bear grinned as Beth reached over and hit Monty on the arm. "I'm not you're squaw," she said. Monty and Running Bear laughed, while the Chief's eyes widened, but said nothing.

Monty pointed toward the steers and said, "We brought you some steers. We have too many. We ask you as our friend to take them to lighten our burden. They are yours to do as you will. With his hand he made jesters toward the small herd. Also we also brought you many gifts for your people. He laid out some blankets, and unrolled them. In side them were knives, rifles, bullets, axes, skillets, and pans. Running Bear said to Monty, "You good friend. Running Bear not forget you."

"Thank you," replied Monty. "You're welcome here anytime. Again, I thank you for your big help with us on the trail. You helped us in delivering our many cows successfully." Monty avoided using any word that would sound like payment. Running Bear laid his long spear, flat side down, on Monty's shoulder and said, "You good friend. We brothers. We hunt, but no game. Buffalo gone, squaws and children bellies empty. Children cry , old ones sing sad song. Monty then motioned to Running Bear to take the cows home." As he told him he smiled . His indian friend then lifted his spear from Monty's shoulder and nodded toward the other indian and his chief and turned his horse toward the cows and the three of them began to move the cows back the way they had come. Monty called out to their chief and Running Bear, as they turned their horses to face him, Monty said, "There's lots of game on our ranch. You're welcome to hunt here anytime. Running Bear nodded and then turned again toward his village. Then the three riders turned and rode back toward the ranch.

Chapter Thirteen

Monty finally had his ranch. His dream was coming true. He had at least twenty five excellent broodmares, promising yearlings, two magnificent stallions, and a small contract with the army. But what he didn't have was a wife, … and a family. He decided he better do something about that… the sooner the better. And Beth was right, without thinking he said out loud, "Six months was a long time to wait. "Yep, Too long," he said out loud! Beth turned her head toward Monty and said, "Too long, for what," she asked?

Monty turned his head and looked at her and said, "I was just thinking outloud."

"Thinking about what? Monty Lane, you just finished a big cattle drive! What are you planning now? What ever it is, you better not plan on being gone anywhere."

"Now what makes you think I would do something like that?"

Beth grinned at him and said, "You're record just isn't too good, Mr. Lane!"

Monty edged his horse closer to her's and reached across for her reins. He pulled her horse to a halt, as she turned her head and looked at him, he leaned toward her and said, "Beth, I'm your's forever. I love you with all my heart! What say we move our wedding date up some?" "Like tomorrow?"

"Tomorrow?" she exclaimed. Monty Lane, we can't do that!"

"Why not? You're here, I'm here. Were the ones getting married. All we need is the parson."

"But, Monty, there's the cake, my dress, people to invite, There's just too many things…too many things."

"Well, don't say I didn't try," said Monty.

With a big grin on her face, Beth said, "Sure you did, Monty, Sure you did."